Shlok's Dad

A Father's Perspective of Parenthood

Vivek Sharma

To Pappa

I could know the value of a father, only years after I lost mine. Missed you most when Shlok was born.

To GBS

Still haven't reconciled to your sudden loss. I miss you every day, but the values you taught me are still very strong.

Contents

Preface

This book is my attempt at introducing the undulating crests and troughs of experiences that parenthood entails. A funny take on parenthood from the father's perspective, peppered with personal experiences, and life's lessons learnt. It mustn't be seen as a pedagogic guide to raising children. I mean this book as a light read to reassure new parents, nudge wannabe or unsure parents; and for fellow parents to smile over similar experiences of seeing their offspring grow up (puke, stumble, stub toes) and reminisce over losing their stuff, sleep, hair, teeth and shit.

Above all, I'd want this book to serve as a legacy to my son, for when it's time for him to decide whether to embark on a voyage to the uncharted waters of fatherhood. I might not be around to guide him then, but he can probably draw from my experiences in seeing him grow. What better to learn from, than your own progenitors' mistakes?

Shlok's Dad

She calls out, "Shlok's Dad?" The words suddenly break my reverie as I find myself in the midst of a cacophonous bunch of pre-schoolers, and an equally loud group of their mothers. What am I doing here? The personal pronoun *I* boldly italicized.

Not many people I knew were as morbidly afraid of children as me, nor as uncomfortable around them. And here, finding myself suddenly hurled amongst a gaggle of scarily loud mischief-mongers, I was feeling somewhat out of place. Time for flashback mode.

My wife Reshma and I were smugly convinced that we were better placed in the category of DINK (which stands for Double Income No Kids). But, in the part of the world that we hail from, parental pressures determine the expansion of one's tribe, so yeah. Back to the story.

Through the teeming crowd of cute dwarves, as I see a smiling knee-high mini-me making his way towards me, I feel a familiar tug at my heart as I hear him say, "Papa I am here."

Oh, that's my son! I'm a father, how could I forget? And I'm here to take him home from his preschool. This is neither the first, nor last, occasion that I have a mild attack of fatherhood amnesia. But then I finally respond to the call from my son and his teacher/dispatcher, "Yes, I am here."

With one hand tightly clasping my index finger, his other hand waving to the teacher. The sipper, hanging from the waving hand by a strap, oscillating like a pendulum, dripping water on the floor in myriad patterns.

As I take further stock of his appearance, his hair dishevelled, snot escaping from a nostril, lips and chin appear sticky with some sweet-smelling sap. His shirt is untucked, a button is hanging loose and almost falling off. Further down, a scraped knee, and oh, a sock is missing. OMG! His mother is going to give me a lot of grief over the missing sock. OCD should be her middle name (initials?), and over this case of the mysteriously missing sock she is going to nag for a week.

Meanwhile, he tightens his grip around my finger as he jumps over and into roadside puddles, splashing muddy water onto my polished office shoes. Yes, this dirty, naughty mini-me is my offspring, Shlok.

Who am I? I am now hardly called anything else in most circles other than my identity as a parent. I am Shlok's Dad!

Kids are Fragile

From afar, I look at lovely you,
And I see a cute bundle of joy,
I'll stay away, coz you smell so 'Eww',
And I might break this little toy.

Growing up in Mumbai, India, as part of a huge joint family, us three siblings and several cousins lived together in a sprawling bungalow. As a young teen, I remember not being very fond of younger kids. I always shirked away from holding my little cousins. My excuse was that if I hold too tight, I might break their limbs or crack their bones. Held too lightly, I ran the risk of them falling down, with the same result - fractured bones. Theirs, to begin with, and subsequently mine, of course. Not only was I wary of handling little children, but I also desisted being anywhere around them, lest I end up hurting them with my clumsiness.

This apprehension of mine was not without reason. I distinctly remember a younger me once running the risk of being jailed, or killed, or both. An older cousin of mine had come visiting for a few weeks, and brought her bonny baby daughter along. When not grabbing everyone's attention with her cute babbling, the baby was bundled up in a tight cloth, well-fed and kept sleeping blissfully. She slept on a heavy mattress placed on the floor, with a protective periphery of large pillows around her.

Those were the days when WWF (now WWE) was popular, and every pillow was like a worthy adversary, fair game for a practice wrestling match! I didn't see my niece sleeping amidst the pillows. To my young mind, so many pillows tidily placed in a circle on a thick mattress was tantamount to an invitation for a wrestling Royal Rumble competition. I began running through my options. I could try a DDT, a Tombstone maybe, and several other finishing manoeuvres. To begin with, I thought I should run into the congregation of wrestler pillows with the famous Macho Man Randy Savage Elbow Drop.

Now imagine this. A burly (ok, fat) teenage boy, beginning his run-up to annihilate the pillows, unaware that an invisibly small kid is cosily sleeping amidst the would-be victims. If it weren't for her protective father, alert to my rush towards the mattress, and stopping me mid-flight into my assault, I'd be writing my memoirs from jail. To this day, I cringe when I recall that incident. I'm thankful that he saved the day, and his daughter. She has grown up to be a lovable, smart young woman, and amongst my most loved people. I told her about that incident recently, though she couldn't get the gravity of that situation and waved away my apology. However, that incident further reinforced my phobia of being anywhere around tiny tots.

This fear of holding little kids remained consistent into adulthood, when I refused to come anywhere close to newborns. When a neighbourhood friend became a father, I tried every possible excuse to avoid seeing his newborn, lest I get cornered into developing my parenting skills by holding the newborn.

"When it is your turn to cradle your own nipper, you'll know exactly how to," said an old hag hospital matron, "Go on, hold the little baby!"

I just shook my head. To my friend's questioning eyes, my clear answer was, "Bro, she's quite an adorable and cute little fledgeling, but don't ask me to touch her if you want her to survive. You do know how clumsy I can get with fragile things. For me, children are like butterflies. I love to see them flitting about, sitting pretty, and looking all cute and beautiful. But I don't like to hold them or touch them, as I might end up hurting them."

Another friend involved me into his family's debate around his choice of electing to not have any children. While his parents were categorical about wanting grandchildren, he felt not obliged to yield to their pressing demands. His wife, poor woman, was torn between love for spouse and respect for parents-in-law.

Fortunately for me, my friend's parents didn't mind me, his unmarried childhood friend, attending what was a heated family argument. Unfortunately for me, knowing my distaste for infants, my friend expected me to advocate on his behalf. My lame squeaks of "But, it's a free country, it's his choice" were politely, but firmly, silenced by his parents, and I became a silent observer thereafter. Traitor, though, is what my friend called me.

His last retort, I remember, went thus, "But Mum, I feel that kids are disgusting. Sticky, licky, colicky, yucky and mucky!"

His mother smiled, closing the argument with, "You are so right, son. Children are all that and much more. But parents still love and nurture their kids, aren't you happy that your father and I didn't think like you?"

This particular friend of mine went on to have three children. Never stopped complaining, yes, but never stopped multiplying. During my own phase of no-child policy, which I have covered in the next chapter, he was the one most eager to push me and my wife into the family way.

Traitor!

Think DINK, Wink

Kids are really good, but for others,
I don't think I want my own child,
I'm happy for all fathers and mothers,
My own life, I'd rather live wild!

I had more or less convinced my wife, Reshma, that we did not want to add on to the burgeoning population crisis the world faced. The least we could do to alleviate the population boom was by not contributing to it!

I'd discovered a new catchphrase on the web: DINK, which stood for Double Income No Kids. It became our oft-repeated answer to the "When?" question thrown at us by old aunties.

My lovely spouse, of course, espoused my logic, and wholeheartedly supported the philosophy: thinking DINK.

With the wife on my side, it was only the rest of the world that I had to contend against. Allying with us, both my brothers said they trusted our judgment.

We were a fairly young couple, well-qualified and upwardly mobile upstarts. We had professional ambitions to achieve, a mortgage to pay, and dreams of travelling the world! This was the assertion I was most likely to fall back upon when my friends questioned me.

"When you are nearing thirty, the lack of pitter-patter of tiny feet is often conjectured as a lack of virility."

I was aghast at this comment from a senior colleague. She was widely considered a broad-minded woman. Her own decision of staying unmarried was widely supported by all her colleagues.

I angrily blurted out, "So just to prove my manliness, you want me to bear steep hospital expenses, and school fees for the rest of my life? There are better ways of proving my manhood, a sperm count test or..." I didn't dare to complete the sentence for my need of a continued career.

Our social circle, meanwhile, was expanding, and not in the way I would have liked it to. So many of our friends, close and distant relatives, even random acquaintances were getting pregnant, I was beginning to think it was a pandemic. My friends, wife's friends, the neighbours, several relatives, it was a deluge of pregnancies. And every bit of news delivered to either my mom or Reshma's mom was met with raised eyebrows.

Reshma and I remained unwaveringly steadfast in our joint decision to remain childless. Till it all changed.

Almost overnight, my partner in crime, and in matrimony, turned coat.

My wife's younger sister informed us that she was about to become a mother. We were all generally very happy for her, but trouble began brewing in my household.

My co-brother summarised the situation pretty well for me, "You must hate me so much, dear brother. In my quest to impregnate my wife, I ended up screwing you pretty bad. I can imagine the pressure you must be facing now to deliver." Very punny, bro.

The murmurs from our mothers were becoming louder and more frequent. Reshma took the intelligent way out, by deflecting. She started directing both of them to speak with me, telling them that I was the one who was insistent on not having children. My mother-in-law desisted from speaking with me on this touchy topic, but my own mother wasn't as charitable.

We didn't have a conversation, it was a monologue by her: "Don't give me this lame argument about financial stability, we weren't exactly billionaires when I gave birth to you. Children are born with their own destiny. And I am not endorsing your silly philosophy of DINK."

The last straw which broke the proverbial back of my wife's resolve was the birth of her sister's son. Cradling the cute little bundle of joy tightly close, she announced, "I want a child of my own, just like him. And I might decide to stop working to become a stay-at-home-mom for my kiddo."

Eventually, sanity prevailed when my wife insisted that she put in a lot of effort in her education and workplace to reach such a senior position this early in her career, and that she still has the drive to contribute to the workforce.

However, with those words: 'stay-at-home-mom', I could see my pet credo of DINK: Double Income No Kids, change into SINK: Single Income, New Kid!

I hate being monotonous, but I will have to end this chapter using the same word I ended the last one with.

Traitor!

We are Pregnant

I'm curious, how would it feel,
To be pregnant, have my own kid,
I can surely, easily with it, deal,
Like countless parents, before me did!

This book is not meant to be a guide on making or getting pregnant, nor is it a tome on surviving pregnancy and childbirth. I am not an expert on the topic, plus there are enough and more books written by experts, so I will not feed you the gory details of what we experienced, and how we went about it. Hence, I'll quickly cut to the chase, to the part after 'WE' got pregnant. Yes, we learnt the term from the several books we had bought on pregnancy and parenting.

Being new-age would-be parents, we had decided to practise inclusive parenting, with both parents being equally involved in the nurturing of our offspring. Not for us the archaic and impractical philosophies of yore where the father only contributed towards the paying of bills, unaware of which school his children went to, or sometimes even their names!

My favourite catchphrase during 'OUR' pregnancy, which I had read somewhere and wholeheartedly adopted, was 'empathy eating'. The concept was, to spare the pregnant woman the guilt of eating for two people, the man too joins her in eating correspondingly copious quantities of food. For every bite Reshma ate, I devoured more, voraciously so. I mean, my poor wife needed that support from her husband, didn't she? Hence, by the start of the third trimester, my baby bump showed more prominently than hers. While she lost the extra weight almost immediately after delivery, more than a decade later I am still struggling to get rid of the vestiges of my misadventures with empathy eating.

With the due date less than three months away, I got a bit apprehensive with the prospect of being in the hospital delivery room. Opinion was divided over whether the man could see so much blood and tears, as we had heard stories of men actually fainting seeing their wives giving birth. To help me decide, I sought advice from a dear friend, who was also my senior colleague. He answered with a simple yes, then related his own experience of seeing his son's birth.

"So dude, it's pretty simple, actually. Let me use a sporting analogy to explain the concept to you. Just imagine watching a cricket match in the stadium, with your wife as the batsman, the doctor the bowler, the head nurse is the fielder. All the other nurses, staff, and you, are simply the spectators. You only need to just cheer and shout. You can probably even take a football game analogy, or any other sport, just understand the concept that you are only the spectator. In my case, all the nurses were screaming my wife's name, 'Nafisa', followed by 'Push, Push.' I joined in on their chants with my louder 'Push, Push.' Then the baby came out, and everyone cheered and clapped. If you can survive watching a sport in a crowded stadium, this is a cakewalk, just less loud and frenzied."

Emboldened by his assurances, and armed with this information, I emphatically declared that I will indeed stand beside my darling wife during childbirth. Looking forward to the mega event, I was even toying with the idea of designing some pretty placards for the event. One witty idea I'd thought for a chant was "Reshma, push Ma."

"So, how long does it take for the child to pop out once she begins experiencing labour pain, Doc?" I asked the ob-gyn (obstetrician-gynaecologist), mighty concerned that my offspring mustn't take birth in the taxi while we traverse through the city traffic.

The doctor smiled, saying that in the first pregnancy the duration of labour lasts for a considerable amount of time, and that we could pretty much travel across continents during that period.

With all my concerns allayed, I began to enjoy the last trimester to the hilt. Meals, of course, were elaborate.

Someone had told us that our social life and all entertainment will be curbed when the baby arrives. So we happily partied with our friends almost every weekend. Plus, we ensured that we caught every movie which was released during that time. Any which movie. Even the flop ones, we'd rather fall asleep in the theatre while watching a boring movie, as we would miss the experience of going to the theatres for a long time coming, right?

False Alarm

Your arrival will send my heart racing,
The promise of your birth, does charm,
But I get scared, around pacing,
When each sign is a false alarm!

One morning, when wifey experienced a little bit of discomfort, I declared a national emergency. We grabbed all the stuff we could and rushed to the ob-gyn, only to be chided over getting worked up over a false alarm. The doctor said we are still a good three weeks away from the due date.

We then made intricate grab-lists and plans, in case the labour pain catches us unawares. I was keen to conduct a 'dry run' to the hospital, to test out our plans and grab-list readiness. BCP (Business Continuity Planning) is a keyword in our corporate organisations, and we wanted to be ready for all eventualities. During one such planning discussion, with the ob-gyn in conference, we weighed the merits of induced labour, C-Section and epidural injections. While the doctor was categorical that he wanted Reshma to deliver naturally, he suggested that we might want to consider an epidural injection to alleviate the labour pain.

A week later, I invited my mom and younger sister-in-law to accompany us for a dry run to the maternity hospital. I wanted them to get familiar with the location of the hospital, and general topography thereabout. The plan was to get a checkup done, recce the place, dine at a nearby restaurant, and watch a newly-released Bollywood potboiler. Before we left for the hospital, Reshma again felt the same discomfort of a week back, which the ob-gyn had adjudged as a false alarm. Great, I said, false alarms warrant a dry run. Due date, of course, was a fortnight away. Our sizeable bag containing all the items on our grab-list was left sitting pretty at home. We didn't want to carry a heavy load for a dry run, and then to the movie.

At the hospital, after a checkup, this time around we were informed that Reshma was already in labour. In denial, Reshma shook her head, convinced that the good doctor was being sarcastic, remembering that we were admonished for overreacting just a week ago.

Reshma asked the doctor's assistant whether we could come back to get admitted, "After some shopping, or maybe even the movie?"

The assistant doctor laughed aloud, but clarified that Reshma cannot be allowed to leave the hospital, and proceeded with the admission formalities. Apparently, the 'slight discomfort' my wife had felt was the onset of early contractions.

The ob-gyn's wife, an accomplished doctor herself, reassured us that labour had just begun, and would last about 10-12 hours or so. She suggested that my mom and sister-in-law go home and rest overnight, asking them to come back early the next morning when the doctor would expect to conduct the delivery. Seeing them leave broke my resolve. I badgered them to stay back, with my pleas falling on deaf ears. Around 8 PM, they left for home.

We were the only couple in the hospital, and had the full attention of the skeletal staff after the doctors left for the evening. They ordered food for us, and left us to enjoy the comforts of the hospital room. Still in disbelief that she was already in labour, Reshma could hardly eat any dinner, while I gorged. To calm her down, the nurse attached on her a contraption, which monitored the foetal heart rate, while also measuring the duration of contractions and the time between them. I'd think this was her earnest way of helping us to hear our baby's heartbeat, and also know that there is still time for the birth.

Most people are accustomed to hearing heartbeats in the vicinity of 60 beats per minute. Maybe a brisk walk takes it to 80-ish. A normal foetal heart rate is double that, around 120-160. We were not aware of that. Yes, I googled this much later. But back then, over the device, to my mind it sounded like a galloping horse, which was getting faster each passing hour.

She Will Kill Me If...

"I love you my darling, so much",
I said, looking at her bearing labour pain,
"You did this to me, just don't touch",
She said, glaring in anger and disdain!

It was a little bit post-midnight, and the loud galloping heartbeats disallowed either of us to sleep. Initially, the nurse kept looking in every hour, but I realised she was coming in more frequently.

She whispered to me, "It seems that the contractions are getting longer, and she is dilating a few centimetres quite some too."

My indignance showed through in my curt response, "With this loud sound of a horse galloping in our room, coupled with her increasingly scary groans of pain, I think I have dilated quite much more."

By another hour, my wife's groans became too loud for me to bear. I thought to myself, that I would definitely not accompany her to the delivery room in the morning.

She decided that she needed to walk, hoping that would dissipate the pain, if not curtail the contractions. It took her barely a few strides when she cried aloud, "Hey, I think my water just broke and I am leaking!"

"Yeah, that happens when you keep gulping water by the litre! You never listen, and now you've peed yourself, whoa, on the hospital floor, how embarrassing!"

"You fucking idiot," she rasped, "My water bag has broken, I am leaking amniotic fluid, call the nurse."

Men, I realised, use cuss words for the fun of it. Women in labour, abuse when they mean serious business.

The maternity hospital's night staff consisted of three people: the nurse, the ward boy, and an apology of a resident doctor. The nurse had to literally shake him to wake him up and get the operation-cum-delivery room ready for us. Meanwhile the ward boy was dispatched on an expedition to fetch the wheeled stretcher. Sizing me up, then deducing that I wouldn't be able to help carry her across the corridor, my brave wife volunteered to walk into the delivery room.

Her screams were now louder shrieks, and gradually becoming deafening howls. Lying on the operating table, she barked instructions at me: to call the ob-gyn, call my mom, call her dad, and call the ob-gyn again.

I had called the ob-gyn four times in a span of ten minutes, and he calmly told me he is on the way all four times. The fifth time I called him, I began with a volley of choicest Hindi cuss words, and again, he calmly responded that he was parking his car.

Meanwhile, I called my mom and my sister-in-law, and begged them to come to the hospital. I was shaken to the core seeing my wife crying in such pain, and feeling quite helpless. I was most wary of calling my father-in-law, who'd entrusted his daughter in my care, and look what I'd done to her!

Reshma refused to leave my hand, which was now throbbing in pain as she squeezed harder each time she had a contraction. I requested her to let my hand free as I had to step away and make a phone call to her dad, since I was wary of him hearing her screams.

"No," she insisted, "I want to hold your hand, call him from right here. You don't need two hands to use your mobile phone, do you?"

Trembling with fear, I dialled the number of the man who loves my wife more than I can ever do, and I asked him to come to the hospital as she was in labour. He sounded groggy but concerned, and asked me who was bellowing loudly in the background, as he could hardly make out what I was saying.

Asking him to please come over to the hospital as his daughter was about to deliver, I promptly disconnected, not wanting to risk coinciding the date of my child's birth with that of my murder.

Speaking of murder, what my wife warned me of next, while lying in the delivery room awaiting the ob-gyn, will remain with me for my lifetime.

"Hear this, asshole, you ask me for another kid, and I will fucking kill you."

It's a Boy!

She cried in pain, the kid too, bawled,
But the others cried out in joy,
I wept too, when the Doc called,
Saying, "You're a Dad, It's a Boy!"

The swinging double doors of the delivery room swung inwards with a whoosh, and the team of the ob-gyn, his wife (also a Doctor), anaesthesiologist, paediatrician, more nursing staff, all walked in, with the sleepy bleary-eyed resident doctor bringing up the rear. I was so relieved seeing the ob-gyn, and suddenly remembered I was primed up for this scenario. This is a stadium, and I am the cheering spectator!

I had only begun to clear my throat for the wild cheering and screaming, when while preparing his surgical equipment the ob-gyn asked my wife to calm down and breathe normally.

"Reshma, don't push," he said, "it is too early, and your child isn't ready to come out yet. Please don't rush the natural process."

Have you ever gone to the stadium, bought premium tickets, only to have the game washed out? I was beginning to feel somewhat similar, with his words having the 'rain on my parade' effect. I've never asked her about this, but I am sure through the cloud of pain, Reshma must have expected to hear my "Reshma, push Ma" instead of what she was just told.

Sporting enthusiasm deflated, I took a few steps back, standing behind the resident doctor, whose expression made me feel like he was just teleported to the hospital in error, and would have preferred to be in a bar, or on a bed. I realised, him and me, we were both looking like we belonged elsewhere. I think I switched off a bit then, and my thoughts wandered.

I began thinking about the months leading up to this moment. In my drive for inclusive parenting, I had done a lot of reading. One particular article I'd read mentioned an interesting research. The researchers had hypothesized that during pregnancy, the father undergoes hormonal changes, making him more sensitive. Apparently, this goes back to our caveman days, when the aggressive alpha male was full of testosterone-driven machismo. But when his cavewoman became pregnant and delivered their child, his hormones changed. Essentially to render him amenable to fatherhood. By making him more nurturing, understanding, protective, sensitive - in one word, motherly. I was hoping this hormonal change business doesn't affect my hair growth, on the head or elsewhere, and leaves my man parts intact. I needed these, of course, to function as a man.

Much later, during a checkup, I'd apologised to the ob-gyn about my cursing on that fateful night, blaming my behaviour to this research finding of hormonal changes.

He replied, "I've delivered countless babies. Your behaviour is exactly how men behave when in panic. Women, on the other hand, are much more composed as they are the stronger gender - physically, mentally, and emotionally."

I was jolted back to the scene when I saw some change in activity at the operating table, though my view was quite obstructed. I'd given up my ringside spot when I moved back at the prospect of not being able to cheer and chant. The ob-gyn, while doing something that surgeons do, was asking my wife to just breathe, breathe, and breathe normally. Suddenly I saw a little body pop out of my wife, and land in the able hands of the doctor. I'd have expected a huge round of applause at the quick reflexes of his catching feat, but he nonchalantly handed the baby (my kid!) to the nurse standing next to him, and carried on with the tasks of what surgeons do. Some bit of cutting, some amount of sewing, and some thingamajig.

My attention moved to the little bundle the nurse was now fussing over. Rubbing, cleaning, vigorously with a towel which was being dipped in hot water (that's what I could make out of it). The nursing staff's increased flurry of activity indicated they were concerned about something. The only word I could make out in their hushed talk was 'breathe'. At this point, the resident doctor - my partner in obsolescence till then - woke up, took charge and told me, "I think you must go outside and wait."

Stepping out, I was getting very anxious. Wasn't my child breathing? I stood just outside the swinging double doors, peering through the porthole-shaped window, my thoughts all muddled up in emotion, my eyes welled up.

Through my tears, I saw the nurses surrounding the head nurse, all cajoling the kid to breathe. The ob-gyn's doctor wife entered the melee, taking the newborn from the head nurse. She held both the child's legs with one hand, my newborn suspended upside down. A resounding slap on the bum next, instantaneously followed by an uproarious cry by the baby. That cry seemed to lighten the mood of the nurses. I felt I could safely breathe again. She handed the crying baby to the head nurse, saw me peering through the window, and walked towards me.

Coming to me, she said, "Congratulations, you are a Dad, to a healthy baby. It's a boy!"

Overcome with a surge of emotions, I swallowed the lump in my throat, "How's... How's my wife doing?"

She replied with a smile, "She's good too, we'll roll her out to the room in a few minutes. Anything else I can help you with, son?"

"Can I get a hug?" was all I could muster up, before falling into her welcome arms and bawling the loudest I've ever bawled since I can remember.

Shape of My Hands

Nothing prepared me for this moment,
I was scared to even hold you, so,
But now I can confidently comment,
Cradling a baby is easy, I told you, so!

I had planned on noting down the exact moment my offspring took birth, both for posterity and astrological reasons, but I was so caught up in the onslaught of different emotions, that it totally slipped my mind. In her situation, I obviously couldn't expect Reshma to keep track of time, so we relied on the hospital's version of the time of birth. The certificate read 2:35 AM, a clear 6-7 hours earlier than the time the doctor had estimated, and a good fourteen days ahead of the original calculation of gestation.

A little bit around 3 AM, my mom and sister-in-law reached. Crying, I hugged both of them tightly, wetting their shoulders while muttering "I am a Dad!"

Before that, with not the slightest of embarrassment I'd already been done embracing all the staff, leaving them with tear-wet sleeves; and later upon their arrival I also hugged my mother-in-law and father-in-law; him with no trepidation.

"It's a boy!" I excitedly told them.

"Is that so? Then please prove it." My father-in-law thundered into the neonatal care room where my son was now transferred into, kept in a small incubator. He insisted on the head nurse unbundling the swaddle to show him the child, stark naked in all his glory. Everyone else found this amusing, though I couldn't see the point in getting the child in the nude, in front of so many prying eyes. Unperturbed, and convinced of the gender of his grandson, he asked them to clothe the child again, proceeding to click pictures of the newborn on his phone camera.

Sensing my discomfort, he placed his hand on my shoulder and explained, "In a country as populous as ours, and more so in a densely-packed city like Mumbai, it is not uncommon for children to get exchanged inadvertently. So it's always better to verify, you see."

I glanced at the empty ward, knowing well that this maternity hospital had only one newborn, and surmised that the gush of motherly hormones hadn't spared my macho father-in-law either.

While everyone else fawned over the baby, I rushed to the delivery room frantically searching for my wife, just to find her being wheeled out on a stretcher. Thankfully, they'd finally found a stretcher by then. Seeing me, Reshma spread her arms out, and pulled me close to her. She wanted to say something to me, but was too weak to say any louder than a faint whisper. She had to repeat thrice before I could make out what she wanted to say.

"Epidural, epidural. Tell the doc I need the epidural injection for the delivery, and call my dad before taking me into the delivery room."

Shifted into the bed, she fell asleep, exhausted, and I sat by her bedside. Just the two of us in the room. I somehow felt this is the only time it will be just the two of us together for a long, long time to come, and I wanted to tend to my sleeping wife, holding her hand. But my mom came to fetch me.

"Hey, come with me. Don't bother her. Let her sleep. I need you to do something for me."

I was apprehensive of the task she was calling me for. My suspicions came true when she ushered me into the neonatal care room where my son was kept in the incubator. She was well aware of my fears of handling a baby, but exhorted me to hold my offspring in my own hands. The scientific explanation, mixed with lore, was that skin-to-skin contact helps in bonding with the baby. While the newborn would get enough and more opportunities to bond with his mother, I was less equipped to feed him naturally.

I was afraid I'd end up dropping the child on the cold, hard floor, but my mother was unyielding, so were my father-in-law, mother-in-law and sis-in-law. Mom showed me how to hold my hands out to receive the baby. With both palms held supine, fingers on the right hand pointing away from the body, and the fingers on the left hand pointed perpendicular towards the right palm, at a distance of a few inches depending on the length of the baby (yes, length, it's called height when they begin to stand upright). It is as much a science as an art, and to this day I end up practising this position before offering to hold any infant.

When I was ready in position to receive him, Mom gently placed him in my arms. He opened his eyes and for a brief moment, our eyes met. A fleeting glance later, he closed his eyes again, and I cradled him closer. Fighting back tears, smiling at the same time, holding him lightly, yet so firmly. Afraid no more, I was now dead sure of one thing, that I won't drop him, or break him. Or allow anything in the world to ever hurt him.

My mom nodded her approval when I said, "It feels like the shape of my hands has been designed only to hold him, and perfectly so. I am not letting go of him now."

Father is Dazed

Becoming a father does, one, astound,
It just leaves you in a bit of a daze,
Today, the feeling is so profound,
My child's birth is my life's best phase!

It was close to daybreak when everyone left for home, to make arrangements for welcoming the child and mother home. My wife and son asleep, I was left to myself. It dawned upon me that I need to inform the rest of the family, my friends and my colleagues about the new arrival.

My broadcast text read thus, "Reshma delivered a baby boy earlier last night. Mom and baby are fine. Father is dazed."

Three of my closest friends arrived within an hour of my sending the message, and I was the first of this close quartet to have become a parent. They expressed a variety of emotions, from disbelief, to happiness, to the realisation that we had, over the course of one night, turned a corner in life; and that we weren't kids anymore.

One of them asked me, "So, how does it feel to be a father?"

"Shell-shocked," I began, "but the feelings are too mixed, maybe I'll be clearer about the feeling later. What I feel is something inexplicable. You know me well, I am usually articulate, but I can't seem to find the right words to define this feeling."

Even a decade since then, when asked this question, I still say the same. As a father you feel responsible, yet useless. Forceful, yet weak. Important, yet inconsequential. Over the years, my child has taught me that parenting life is brimming with many such oxymorons. You'd have felt happy tears pre-parenthood, but can experience happy anger with a kid. You learn that you can be firm without being loud. Or the sheer heart-wrenching feeling of wanting to spoil your kid crazy, yet denying some of their demands just to build their character. Like my wife says, being a parent makes one feel like kissing and killing at the same time.

Paeans have been written in the glory of the mother, epics composed about the unconditional love of a mother, the wondrous feelings motherhood lends. Even patriarchal societies place the position of a mother at a higher pedestal than the position a father enjoys. No poet has knitted pearls of words in the praise of a father. I fully endorse that the role of a mother holds (slightly, ok) more credence than that of a father. But yes, I firmly believe that fatherhood cannot be expressed in words, it is a feeling, an emotion, which can only be experienced. Exactly how I felt the night my son was born.

We were sitting in the visitor's hall, sprawled out on the sofas. Excusing myself, I went to the room to check out on Reshma. She was still in light sleep, so I slinked out in a couple of minutes, not wanting to disturb her. Passing through the corridor, I let myself into the neonatal care room, and lifted my son into my arms again. With no audience, I felt more at ease, rocking him slightly, caressing his feet gently. At that moment, I missed my own father a lot. I'd never managed to reconcile with losing him abruptly to an accident. Years had passed since, and life was so demanding that I could never properly grieve his death. Loss of a parent, at any age, leaves a huge lacuna in life, and is an irreparable loss indeed. Only when you become a father, they say, is when you really begin appreciating your own father, understand his perspective, his firmness, and appreciate your father's tough love. It was a sombre, solemn moment, cradling my newborn son, and missing my father.

I was also missing my maternal uncle, who was a father figure to me. He was my guiding light, and my moral compass. Him too, I'd lost to an untimely death, a very heart-breaking one. I wished he were around with me when I became a father.

A little while later I placed my sleeping son back into the incubator, and walked towards the glass wall separating the nurses' chamber from the neonatal care room. Overcome with a deluge of emotions, I leaned against the glass wall, and began to weep. Suddenly, my friend tapped me on the shoulder, "Dude, are you okay? What are you doing here, all alone, and watching...?"

I wiped my tears away, meaning to apologise to him and explain to him the research findings about hormonal changes brought about by childbirth, "I know, these raging hormones..."

He interjected, "Yes, Bro, I can understand that. I was just getting to know that pretty nurse when we saw you peeking into the chamber through the glass, looking at her, at us. You, I mean, me, I mean... She is hot, eh?"

Dazed, exactly.

Shit Happens, or Doesn't

Earlier the questions were pretty simple,
Whether one drinks or eats, soup?,
Now they ask, with a wink and dimple,
Does soup come out as pee, or poop?

Later that morning, my three best friends and I saw the morning-shift nurse taking my son, undressing him and placing him in a bath sink (it pretty much looked like a regular kitchen sink to my untrained eyes). While we watched my newborn son being administered his first bath, another friend ambled up close behind us, and smilingly exclaimed, "Oh wow, nice, congrats... and hey, look at this cute little piece of black shit."

We collectively glared at him, and fearing that he was in mortal danger of being lynched by not one, but four of his dear friends, he meekly explained, "Brothers, I was just talking about meconium, a baby's first poo. It's an indication that the child's digestion is working normally. It is indeed tar-like in colour and consistency."

He immediately pulled up his shirt showing us some scars, explaining that he had to be operated upon in infancy, apparently because he had not passed out meconium, which consists of mucus, amniotic fluid and everything that the foetus ingests while in the womb.

If you scroll through any parents' forum on the internet, you'll find pages and pages that are devoted to poo. Parenting books have chapters which are dedicated to bowel movements, and what is construed as normal function. You chat with any new mother about her little one, and invariably she will speak about the colour of their offspring's poop. My wife was part of a 'new mothers' group on Facebook, and mothers in that group got elated or worked up about the regularity and volume of their child's shit. Pandemonium erupts when a child doesn't poop for even a couple of days, with corresponding outpour of relief when the kid eventually does pass some crap.

We, too, have been equally culpable, if not more. Our child's stools were national news for us. One week of no pooping would drive us crazy with calls to our respective mothers, who would offer grandma's 'secret sauce' remedies. When he'd poop eventually, we would broadcast it to the extended family and all our friends about the texture and consistency of the faeces. As if anyone else was really that much interested; disgusted more likely.

Thankfully, it was not just Reshma and I who were obsessed with his poop. Let me take you on a quick trip of potty-related memories with my son at different ages. Once, when he was a little over two years old, my mom made an emergency call to Reshma and me in our offices. Apparently, Shlok was trying to pass some stool but couldn't. We were summoned to take him to the paediatrician. The three of us bundled into a cab, en route to the doctor. He insisted on standing the entire thirty-minute drive to the clinic. I was still unaware of the exact nature of the emergency, so I asked Shlok what exactly was bothering him.

He said, in the cutest of children's lisp, "Coz my potty is hanging in my bum bum."

I couldn't control my laughter, while my wife angrily lambasted me for laughing at the misfortune of our own flesh and blood.

The potty issue doesn't end with whether it happens or not. Often there are larger issues to contend with, around what is to be done after it happens. Domestic wars have erupted over cleaning up after a child has done the potty thing. Mothers have a plausible contention that they take care of the input end by donating their milk into it, the least the fathers can do is take care of the output end. Fathers' protests are mostly considered inadmissible.

It takes a lot of dexterity with the equipment, military precision to avoid any spills, manoeuvring deftly, with the kid seeming intent to kick the soiled nappy, all the while holding your breath lest the waft of the toxic stuff kills you.

I too, have had to deal with the ignominy of having to use wet wipes, apply powder, replace the nappy, essentially go through the entire process without inasmuch taking a breath. However, I survived, did it just that once, got my bravery award, and promised myself to defer repeating it till eternity.

In some time, my son also understood that cleaning up after a crapping kid requires training, and is an acquired skill. On one occasion, when he wanted to go to the toilet when Reshma was in office, my sister-in-law volunteered to help her three-year old nephew out. She encouraged him to not feel shy and go on.

His earnest query was, "I really want to go number two, but you sure you know how to (clean up)?"

A few years later, I asked six-year-old Shlok what his opinion was about why humankind decided to clean up after taking a crap, as opposed to animals.

His guess was, "If we don't clean up after we shit, our pants would get dirty, that's the only reason I can think of."

I am not even touching upon the universal debate on washing versus wiping after doing one's night soil business, else we risk this book running into reams of paper, which might end up being put to that precise use.

While in public everyone expresses abhorrence for toilet humour, all parents have their own secret stash of potty jokes, with which they regale their family and close friends; all at the expense of, and embarrassment to, their innocent children. Children's pee-and-poo accidents and skid marks are part of folklore in every family, but kept guarded like national secrets from outsiders.

We too, have many more of our own inside jokes and horror stories involving our son's bodily functions. We often laugh over them, but seldom do so in polite company.

In private, Reshma accuses that Shlok enjoys it most when I crack jokes involving shit, pee, or farts.

However, coming back to the story, I have never seen before or thereafter, since seeing my son's first poop, five full-grown adult men observing, explaining, getting excited about, and celebrating a 'freshly-delivered' child's 'freshly-delivered' little black turd.

The Global Conundrum

From 'I don't want any kids, not even one',
To having a child, now give me an indication,
Should I give all love to my only son,
Or do I add more to the world's population?

By the time my friends left, both my brothers had arrived at the hospital, with my sister-in-law (my eldest brother's wife) in tow.

I call my elder brother 'Panda', and my eldest brother 'Buzz'. Their arrival gave me the much-needed sense of relief I was probably seeking all night. My siblings brought with them the familiar fraternal assurance, and also some monetary assistance. The latter was critically required, if I wanted to get my wife and newly-arrived son discharged by paying the hospital dues.

I must now digress again, to address the issue after which I've named this chapter. I've always been amongst the youngest in the extended family, leaving out a few much-younger cousins. In fact, some of my cousins were so much older than me, that their children were barely a few years younger to me. Being the kid brother, I always felt the sense of being sheltered, which is afforded to the youngest siblings. On the contrary, my wife is the oldest in her entire clan of siblings and cousins. Both our families are pretty big. I have two elder brothers; she has two younger sisters.

Our parents have an even larger sibling count. My dad had two brothers and three sisters, the last of whom took birth just a few months before Buzz was born. My mom was born as the youngest sibling to one sister and four brothers. My younger aunt was born a couple of years after my mom, taking their count to seven siblings. Since the concept of nuclear families was unbeknownst to folks back then, my mom grew up with a total of fourteen children under the same roof. Reshma's parents too, come from similarly large families.

Essentially, both Reshma and I come from large extended families. Hence, many eyebrows were lifted when Reshma and I announced our one-child policy. And it was not only our immediate circle of family and friends who were concerned, but these following comments also came from people whom we barely knew!

"How can you deprive your child the comforts and support system of his siblings, when you yourself enjoy the same?"

"He'll be all lonely when he's grown up, and you are dead and gone."

"Bah, friends aren't the new family, that's all humbug. Blood is still thicker than water."

"The problem with society is that educated people are having fewer kids, while those wretched illiterates breed like rabbits!"

"Promise me this, once you are back home, you'll begin making another baby with your wife."

This last one came from a well-meaning and sweet Australian woman, who I'd just met when we'd worked together on building houses for villagers, while volunteering in Cambodia.

Even during a subsequent visit to the ob-gyn, he had suggested to us that we must plan a second one quickly, and not space out our children by too much. We politely declined. This was the same visit during which I sheepishly apologised to him for my earlier misdemeanour. Hence, I couldn't afford being blunt in my response to him.

People on both sides of this global debate have quite strong views on this very emotional topic. Each side takes serious umbrage at the arguments the other side considers extremely relevant.

I see, acknowledge, understand and respect both sides of the argument. There are people I love and adore who subscribe to the dogma of having multiple children. People I respect reside on the other side of the spectrum too.

We don't claim to have a solution to this seemingly global conundrum, and prefer to sit on the fence on this one. We can obviously see the merits of having siblings, from our own upbringing. On the flip side, we do understand the logic of devoting all resources towards one child rather than distributing them over two or more offspring.

I suspect children too have strong opinions for and against sharing their bed and parents with someone else. I have heard horror stories of fathers being hit in the crotch, as a painful indicator that their children don't want them copulating anymore. I neither confirm nor deny that similar assaults have happened to me.

Some children see their friends having the company of their siblings, while they return to empty homes, and yearn for a little brother or sister.

This once happened to Shlok too. He was five when he came to me and said he wants a sibling. I welcomed the frank dialogue, with my wife listening in the background. I asked him whether his preference would be a brother or a sister. He mulled over it for a couple of minutes before replying that he'd prefer a brother. I could see my wife getting uncomfortable with this conversation, but I winked at her, a sign that I have this under control.

I probed further, "Do you want a brother for sure? You'll need to share your toys, and maybe bed?"

When I caught him on an unsure footing, I went for the sucker punch, "How about a dog, would you prefer a dog over a brother?". His eyes shone like light-bulbs, and he began to nod vigorously. The negotiations went on for a little bit more, ending with us settling for a Lego set.

When pushed into a corner about my aversion to adding to my tribe, I usually rely on my favourite repartee, "Do you know what's the best measure of birth control? It's School Fees!"

What's in a Name?

What I call my child, who chooses?,
I will name him as per my choice,
But my better half refuses,
Want to pick the name, says a louder voice!

Our return from the hospital was met with a mini festival back home, at our suburban abode. My mom had engaged a professional videographer to capture the momentous memory of her grandchild entering home for the first time.

He was being treated like a celebrity, because he was now the youngest in both Reshma's and my family, I could see him take over the mantle of being the most pampered in my immediate clan. Sibling rivalry I've dealt with, but how does one grapple with competing with your son for your own mother's attention? As with most other things, we soon fell into a semblance of normalcy; call it pecking order if you may.

"So, have you and Reshma agreed on a name for the kid?" asked Panda one lazy weekend afternoon.

I winced. Why to bring up contentious issues when I want to enjoy the lull of the weekend by falling into a siesta? I lobbed the ball back right into his court, before turning over to feign sleep, "Why don't you suggest a few options, you're his uncle after all."

By now everyone had their own favourite 'pet' names to address the little one as. I myself had a list of fifteen random names which I addressed my son as.

However, the birth certificate, school entry, and the passport can only afford one first name; and naming a child is a matter of great deliberation. Most cultures of the world have elaborate naming ceremonies for children, signifying the importance a name carries.

I'd been putting off this naming discussion with my wife, expecting a big showdown on the issue. As usual, she chose the most inopportune time to broach the topic: while I was watching a very important and close game of cricket. She has a killer sense of timing, my wife.

"We can't keep calling him Chhotu all his life, we need to search for and agree upon a good name." 'Chhotu', is a Hindi pet name translating to 'little one'.

"Uh, yeah," I mumbled, while trying to concentrate on the match, "but let him choose the name he prefers, when he is a bit older."

A young woman very close to me, was considered quite a prodigal child. When she was a toddler, her parents named her Kritika. She mispronounced this as Kuttika (which, in Hindi, loosely translates to: 'of a B*tch').

To counter this, her parents pulled out another trump card of a name, Sakshi. Promptly her toddler lisp turned this name to 'Sexy'.

Exasperated, her parents began searching for a new name, and in the interim continued to call her the ubiquitous Chhotu. Nothing to be ashamed of. Youngest children in Indian families are pretty accustomed to being called Chhotu all their lives. Yours truly, too, spent a major portion of life being called thus. Buzz still calls me Chhotu, pretty tolerable compared to the borderline and outright racist name-calling Panda indulges in.

Anyways, ~~Kritika~~ ~~Sakshi~~ Chhotu helped solve the naming troubles of her parents by suggesting a name which she could pronounce well. She decided to name herself Amisha. Pure genius, she is.

"So, it is settled then," my wife continued as I remained transfixed by the ongoings in the cricket game, "as agreed, I will have our spiritual guru suggest a good name for our dear son. You agreed, remember this, ok?"

Decision-making is unilateral in our household. Catch the husband at a time when he is fully concentrating on a sporting event, and he will plain nod. Then you can hold it against him for the rest of his life, saying that a nod is indeed a tacit agreement.

Meanwhile, unaware of said agreement, I put a post on social media seeking inputs from our larger social circle on suggested names. Creative Panda too, upon my earlier

45

request, came up with some funny, villainous, and rather legendary names.

So now we had a bucketful of name suggestions. Some of these carried a risk, as not taking their suggestions for my child's name, might end up offending a few of the proposers. Very difficult path to tread on, this parenthood. Something as simple as naming your child becomes a matter of life and death, risking egoistic snubs and sometimes even social ostracism.

"He has your family's last name, so it's only fair that I get to give him his first name" my wife came with her logical claim on the naming game.

I caught my wife during her weak moment: while she prayed. I retorted to her above line saying, "It's but fair that if he carries my family name, then he carries a name of my choice. So it is settled."

She angrily waved me away, and to my mind, that was tantamount to relenting.

Amongst the several comedic and villainous names Panda had suggested, I found a gem. Shlok, the name struck a chord, and when I suggested it to several people, including my wife, it wasn't opposed too vehemently. Shlok, in Hindi, means hymn, or prayer.

Buzz did disapprove of our choice of name, but I tried placating him. We eventually stuck with Shlok. But not without a lot of further 'due diligence'.

Several benign words in one language actually mean something entirely inappropriate, risqué or even ribald in another language. My interest in linguistics has led me to have enough fodder on the topic for another book.

"Be careful of what you name him, Sir," an office colleague cautioned me, "better to research carefully on the international implications of the name. Who knows, maybe if your son goes abroad for education, his name mustn't be a cause for embarrassment to him."

I fully endorse this opinion. A cousin of mine who stays in the US, actually ran a survey on his office colleagues' ability to pronounce names he'd shortlisted for his son, to ascertain which Indian name would be found most easily pronounceable by the Americans.

There's a reason that people in India, post the advent of internet porn, have stopped naming their sons Anal. Yes, exactly that. The name actually means 'fire' in Sanskrit, and I suggest you Google the meaning of this name in some other geographies too.

Another good example being the name Gopi. I won't spoon feed this one to you. If you didn't get the joke the first time, try breaking the word into syllables, slowly, and try to discover the English transliteration.

India is a huge country, where language changes every 200 kilometres. One also needs to be careful that one isn't selecting a name for their child something which might be inappropriate in another Indian language. It's not just first names, even surnames become an issue sometimes. There are some names and surnames, which take an entirely different meaning in other languages, and must always be avoided, I was cautioned. There are actually some people in India with family names which are spelt Boob, and even Butt.

A good friend of mine, whose surname is Mahadik, faced a lot of ragging during his college days. He'd landed a spot in a prestigious engineering institute in Southern India. He told me that he had to endure a lot of ribbing due to his family name. 'Maha' is a Hindi prefix meaning 'huge', so his Hinglish-speaking seniors drew phallic connotations; with 'Hinglish' being a combination of Hindi and English. More examples, if cited here, would result in an automatic R21 rating for this book. Search the internet, if inquisitive.

"Not only in western and other Indian languages, my friend, you also need to be wary of mispronunciations in local languages, else his friends at school will tease him to no end," informed another very good friend, "My son hates me for naming him what I did. If only I had been careful about choosing his name, he wouldn't have borne the brunt of such insensitive jokes." I couldn't understand for the life of me, why his son's name Sandesh (meaning 'message' in Hindi), should lead to any embarrassment. That was till he himself explained to me that his son's friends often mispronounced his name as Sandaas, which means toilet/crap. Of course, boys and their affinity for toilet humour.

It's not only Indian names which can lead to funny reactions elsewhere in the world. Some of the names I heard while travelling in Thailand would evoke guffaws in the western world for how those names sound in English, and even in rural India for how they sound in Indian languages.

As a reverse example, I would recommend against women named Randi spelling their name out too liberally while travelling in South Asia.

It All Goes Downhill

Giving a child a healthy upbringing,
Is not only all games, and fun,
The child needs lots of nurture, loving,
Also milk, and a lot of sun!

I n a couple of weeks since coming home, we noticed that Shlok wasn't gaining weight, and had also lost some of the reddish-pink colour he was born with. While most newborns lose around 7% to 10% of their birth weight, they regain and even surpass that in a few weeks' time.

Parents obsess over their infant's weight even more than their own. We took Shlok to the paediatrician who gave us the normal weight loss snippet of information. She also said that it's normal for newborns to develop jaundice, and it tends to resolve on its own in a few days.

Considering Shlok's rapid weight loss and persistent jaundice, she recommended phototherapy. In phototherapy, the child is placed in a special bed under a blue light (or so it looked like to me). Although the skin needs to be exposed to the light, the eyes need to be protected by special goggles. Little Shlok looked like a biker in diapers when in that bed.

Someone joked, drawing a parallel to vain women who paid good money in spas for such light therapy, but Reshma failed to see the humour in it. She was just about discharged from the hospital, and now bundled back into another hospital. Uncertainty regarding her son's recovery, coupled with postpartum depression, was taking a toll on her. Furthermore, weakness in a child is often blamed on the mother, and some relatives had made uncharitable comments when Reshma was within earshot. She took to praying even harder, more frequently, fervently hoping that the almighty would help her son gain health and weight. I was blissfully ignorant of the travails she was battling with.

I was very concerned about Shlok's weight though. A senior colleague of mine, seeing me tensed, assured me that underweight infants eventually grow up to be roly-poly kids, mostly because their parents overcompensate for their initial low weight.

We were relieved to see the phototherapy sessions bearing some positive results. Once done with those, the paediatrician told us that natural sunlight would also prove to be helpful. This part of the therapy was entrusted to me. Shlok and I then began a nice daily ritual. At around 4 PM every day, I would lay him, undressed, on my bare torso, and expose him to sunlight through a window.

While he would be peacefully asleep through our daily sunbathing sessions, I ended up understanding the logic behind skin-to-skin bonding which was recommended with the infant. I really enjoyed this exclusive time with Shlok, till time ran out and I needed to resume office.

When not asleep on my torso, Shlok would mostly be tightly bound in a swaddle. I'd read that being swaddled gives infants a sense of security and comfort, which they'd felt while in the womb. Interestingly, Shlok would always manage to get one hand free, even in the tightest of snug swaddles. Resembling the outstretched hand of Superman as seen in some illustrations, I called this hand-freeing action of Shlok as his 'Houdini Trick'.

While otherwise he was pretty angelic in behaviour, except when he was hungry or needing a change of clothes. He would then cry loud enough to wake up the dead, and revert instantly to angel mode when fed and changed.

I'd comment to anyone willing to listen, that I found his sleeping on my chest very therapeutic as a father, and that my swaddled son is an angel. A neighbour who is an experienced father several times over, smirked and said, "A sleeping child is an angel at any age, but you must enjoy these days when he is swaddled. Trust me, the brats are most manageable at this age. It all goes downhill from here." In retrospect, I agree with his last sentence. Truer words were never spoken.

What Goes In, Comes Out

It's so dirty, so messy, and so gross,
Of a child if that's your choice of rebuke,
Your views are only your own loss,
If you can't see the lovely kid beyond the puke!

Shlok and Reshma were now back home, and regaining health. This meant that we had to get ready for an endless stream of visitors. I had to begrudge these callers as they meant well, intending to bless the newborn and congratulate the parents. My mom also encouraged us to begin attending social events, as that would help the child become comfortable amidst strangers.

Shlok had begun to feed well, both mother's milk and formula. We weren't at all ready though, for the issue of regurgitation, also called infant reflux. Upon every feeding, he would unfailingly throw up. It was no mean smell, this curdled milk, trust me.

Google, the parenting help books, our advisors, the paediatrician, all suggested a solution to help him digest milk faster. Explaining to us patiently, the paediatrician said that as grownups, we spend most of our time upright, helping gravity pull the food we eat in the intended direction. In infants, since they spend most of their time lying down, some of the food has a tendency to be regurgitated, often because of overfeeding or air swallowed during feeding.

As part of the solution, after a feed, either Reshma or I (mostly me), would hold Shlok against us, upright, with his chin nestled on our shoulder, patting his back repeatedly, walking around.

Invariably, our little one would promptly throw up on our shoulder and contentedly go back to sleep, leaving us dripping and smelly. Bright enough to hurl clear of himself though. Reshma had developed a defence mechanism to this, she would drape a towel over her shoulder. Me, I never used any such armour, so 2 AM showers were the rule. Over time, several of the clothes we'd wear at home reeked of vomit.

Even our visitors bore the imprint of Shlok's reflux. They were often stamped with approval, and carried back the distinct perfume of 'Being Shlok'.

Around that time, we were invited to my colleague's housewarming party. We were hesitant to attend, as we were apprehensive that Shlok might throw up in their new home. But my mom insisted that we take Shlok along and not be overanxious parents. For such social outings with the kid, Reshma had bought a 'Diaper Bag' to carry a long list of kid's stuff. She often packed in enough stuff in the bag to survive an apocalypse, and I was appointed to lug that bag.

Off we went to the party. Mom, dad, son and diaper bag. Looking as if we were going to settle into my colleague's new house, bringing such a big bag along.

Once there, I was keen to leave at the earliest, just to ensure that my son doesn't take a feed there. I shared my apprehensions with my colleagues, who scolded me, saying it's a natural phenomenon. They gave me good reminders of their own throwing up in front of me when drunk, and being totally unapologetic about it. Feeling better, I gave the green signal to Shlok's feeding.

One of my sweet colleagues volunteered to hold him upright and help him burp. Predictably so, Shlok hurled all over his white shirt, and part of it also found its way onto the new Persian rug the new homeowners had bought. Even if it wasn't Persian, it must have still cost a bomb. I felt so embarrassed, despite the reassurances offered by everyone in attendance there.

To this day, I feel guilty about my son vomiting on my colleague's white shirt. Reshma and I left the party heavy-hearted. Shlok and the diaper bag, I am sure, felt lighter.

It took Isaac Newton to teach us that, "What goes up must come down," but as every parent can explain with confidence, that what goes in, must come out, one way or the other.

Milk of Amnesia

Oh, you, how can I ever forget,
Only think of you, I would rather,
But slip out of mind, oft I let,
That you're born and I'm a father!

While my little one was struggling with keeping milk inside his tummy, I was struggling to keep something inside my brain. Him. I would keep forgetting about him altogether.

No, I am not referring to the frequent cases we hear, of parents forgetting their children in parked, hot cars. I have myself been a victim of something similar.

My grandfather, a religious, devout man, would visit several temples across Mumbai as part of his daily routine. One day, he'd taken little me along for a temple tour across town, far from the suburbs where we lived.

Apparently I was tired with the temple run, so he asked me to sit at the steps of a temple, and await him while he visited an adjacent temple. Immersed in his thoughts and prayers, he forgot all about me, only realising much later in the evening that he'd left me at the temple.

He immediately called one of his business associates who came to retrieve me at the temple, rescuing me from a future of begging for alms at the temple.

I didn't suffer such lapses, thankfully. I am talking about the harmless, temporary amnesia, where I would forget that I had become a parent, that I had a son. In conversations sometimes, I'd still be mentioning that Reshma and I didn't have a child yet. Almost nine months of pregnancy, and a memorable childbirth experience, all forgotten.

Not that my amnesia wasn't dangerous for my kid. I wasn't used to sharing my bed space with a small infant. Late one night, when we were all asleep, Reshma was awakened by what she calls as "mother's instinct", and found my hand placed on her swaddled son's face. Shlok was apparently struggling to breathe, while I was blissfully asleep. When she woke me up, I pretended to have been caressing his cheek, but in all honesty I wasn't aware there was a little one lying right next to me. That was when Reshma decided that Shlok should sleep in the crib.

My fatherhood amnesia continued during waking hours, though. It didn't help that Reshma and Shlok went to her parents' place for a while. My parents-in-law stay in a tony suburban neighbourhood, in another part of Mumbai. Close to two months that they spent there, helped Shlok bond well with his maternal grandparents. He was showered with endless love by his grandfather, who can never see any wrong in anything that his grandson does. Shlok's loving grandmother, religious and patient, prayed for his well-being. As a result of all these prayers and love, Shlok's health gained quite a lot while with them. However, his bonding with me got affected somewhat, my amnesia about having become a parent worsened.

When Shlok and Reshma returned home, my niece came up with a splendid suggestion. She said that in order to acclimatise with parenthood, I should probably go out for walks with my son. The more time I spend with him, only with him, will help father-son bonding, as well as serve as a reminder to me of my fatherhood status.

It was a good idea. I often left with Shlok for a stroll in the evenings, to parks, malls, and the neighbourhood. I soon realised that kids, like puppies, can serve as excellent magnets for female attention. At least when not throwing up. I am not handsome like Adonis, I never was. So I welcomed this new attention I was getting from women all around.

Women of all ages would get instantly attracted to the gurgling kid, and I would enjoy the reflected glory. This would often lead to conversations around how old he is, his name, how cute he looks, how much he resembles me, how much they adore an indulgent father.

Even when we were out somewhere with my wife around, I'd insist on pushing Shlok's little stroller, loving the approving glance of my wife, and obviously those of other women around.

My sister-in-law once told Reshma, "Look at how he enjoys being surrounded by women, flirting nonchalantly. He has made his son his wingman. Good strategy!"

My wife just winked, "Basking in reflected glory! Let him enjoy the attention while it lasts. Shlok will soon grow out of the 'cute little baby' phase, and my husband will lose his 'chick magnet' charm. For his own good though, while striving to overcome his amnesia of becoming a father, I hope he doesn't end up forgetting that he is married!"

Motor Skills

They keep feeding and sleeping mostly,
Then quickly learn to crawl, walk and run,
Missing seeing these landmarks, prove costly,
Seeing your child grow is a lot of fun!

C hildren are naturally curious, and try to gravitate towards articles they find interesting. In most cases, the object of their curiosity, when out of reach, is immobile and doesn't come running to them. Hence, they themselves try to move towards it.

With Shlok, he called out to things with animated gestures and "Ayeee, Uhhhh" sounds, but inanimate objects never responded to his calls. Lying pretty on his custom-made mattress, he invited the crows, the ceiling fan, even items hung to dry on the clothesline. But his calls weren't reciprocated. So he made futile attempts to either call louder, or move closer. The latter became possible as he gained a bit of motor skills.

However, he was ill-equipped to navigate beyond a few inches. One day we heard him whimpering, and rushed to check on him. He was at the edge of the mattress, holding the mattress cover very tightly, balancing tentatively. He was apparently afraid that he would fall on the ground, as the mattress was a lofty (for him!) two inches from the floor. It was a laughing matter to us, but for him, hanging on to dear life, it was definitely an issue of survival.

Once our little one got the hang of moving around, it became difficult to keep him in one place anymore, his curiosity taking him every which place. Before he mastered crawling on all fours, though, he had a manoeuvre we had no words to explain. With one hand pointing in the intended direction of movement, he would drag himself using his other hand, with the legs putting in the bottom-end part of the work. I coined a term, 'wounded soldier move', as that was the closest resemblance to anything explicable.

We had to babyproof the entire house in order to defend against the attacks of the wounded soldier. Access to the bathroom was barricaded. All low-lying electrical outlets had to be covered. Soon he learnt how to crawl as well.

Shlok's crawling phase was a fun game for me. My mom observed that instead of going around obstacles (like pillows, rolled up rugs, other paraphernalia) he preferred to go over them. She predicted that he'll excel at hurdle races. So, I would set up an obstacle course for him, and he relished every challenge I made for him.

Every parent wants to see for themselves their child's list of firsts. I'd beaten Reshma at seeing Shlok poop for the first time, but she saw him stand up by himself for the first time. In his attempt to reach the bathroom, he had tried to go under the barricade, which had proved impossible, so he pulled himself up using the barricade's bars. With a wide smile, he looked at Reshma like he'd won an Olympic gold. Reshma and Shlok orchestrated an encore of this feat for me when I came home that evening.

Walking was then just a natural progression. Stand up, look at how the elders do it, try putting one foot ahead of the other, that is how we ambulate. However, on several occasions he forgot the golden rules and fell flat, on his face sometimes. To encourage him to walk, and to avoid injurious falls, I would place both my hands on his shoulders while he safely walked around the apartment, with me making 'vroom vroom' motorcycle sounds.

However, I couldn't be around all the time to keep him safe from falling. This led to him being bought a walker to help him attain finesse in the art of walking.

His newly-mastered motor skills made him naughty. Once he learnt how to latch and unlatch doors, it was tough to keep him from mischief. My mom had a harrowing half an hour one afternoon when Shlok locked her inside the bathroom. All she could do was wait for someone to rescue her, while her impish grandson was laughing on the other side of the door. We had to get the door latches reattached higher beyond his reach.

Walking accomplished, he next wanted to step out of the door. Which involves footwear. He didn't understand

61

the concept of different foot sizes, and took a fancy to my office shoes. We'd often catch him wearing my office shoes, and seemingly ready to walk out and conquer the world, wearing a smile, office shoes and a diaper.

Baby Talk

My kid speaks a babbling tongue,
Mostly all words he spouts are gibberish,
Don't judge me, by being high-strung,
As I join in the babble, then look sheepish!

While he was on his way to learn walking, we were pretty dismayed that Shlok hadn't begun talking as yet. Yes he would smile, laugh; and crazy laughter at that. He would even scream his lungs out when crying. But words, it seemed, never escaped those lips.

We had read those parenting books which dictated specific ages at which certain milestones should be achieved. Google scared us further. We were really worried about our child's development. Reshma went eagerly to her spiritual guru, to seek his blessings for our son to begin talking. He blessed her, but jokingly asked her to be careful what she wished for, as once her son started talking, Reshma would soon seek blessings to make him stop talking.

Buzz once took me aside, when he heard me carp about Shlok missing the timelines for talking.

"Your fears don't need to be impressed on the little one. He cannot speak yet, but he can surely see and hear. Be careful with your behaviour and your words around him," he reprimanded me, "Why must he comply with what all those books say? Should books dictate how he must grow?"

"Every child is different, and must be allowed to grow and learn at their own pace. He'll speak when he wants to speak. You mentioned the average age for milestones, bro, what's the relevance of average in a world full of individuals? If our parents had access to Google, or had read those parenting books you refer to, trust me even we'd have not been labelled as normal!"

We still tried to search for ways of coaxing him to talk, or even babble. My mom had discovered that Shlok was very possessive about his tiny feet. We would hold his feet, covering the toes. He would smile, then move our hand away, and check whether his toes were intact. The ploy didn't work in making him utter a word of protest.

However, the moment of joy eventually came. I was rocking his cradle one day, and he'd frown when I stopped rocking. I offered him a deal: that I'd continue rocking if he said something. Anything. He smiled, appearing to me that he understood. Parting his cute little lips apart, my son said to me, "Agoo!"

Ecstatic, I called my wife and mom into the room, egging Shlok on to repeat the magic word. Round eyes stared back at me, as if I were the one babbling. Thankfully though, in a little while he again said his 'Agoo', and louder this time, convincing my mom and wife that I wasn't going gaga.

Soon, we began recording his 'Agoo' sounds and sharing with the rest of the family; everyone gushing about how cutely he curled his lips, trying different pronunciations of the word. Indeed, 'Agoo' sometimes sounded 'Aye-goo', 'Ah-goo', 'Er-Gyu'. You catch my drift, right?

It wasn't just Reshma and I, our family members too shared Shlok's 'Agoo' videos widely, while speculating over what that word might mean in baby speak.

Shlok started having longish conversations with his toys, them listening in rapt attention while my son waxed eloquent in words from his newfound babbling vocabulary. When at home, I'd join in on some of these toy conferences, often speaking to, and sometimes on behalf of, the toys. Reshma had secretly recorded videos of a couple of such toy-conferences, ribbing me to no end and threatening to post the videos on social media.

When your child begins babbling, you do so too, much to the irritation of non-parents. We all know how new sweethearts address each other with such lovey-dovey names. Jaanu, Babu, Pookie, Boo Boo, maybe Tootsie? Sounds about as appealing as fingernails on a chalkboard.

Well, parents of babbling kids take this to the next level of inanity. Words, which might seem unpronounceable in all tongues, suddenly start to carry a meaning. Especially when it evokes laughter or a similar response from the child.

Baby talk is often combined with hugely exaggerated facial expressions that would put Jim Carrey to shame. Let's just say that such behaviour, if not in the vicinity of a toddler, would warrant immediate straitjacket and commitment into a mental asylum.

Reshma was the one lucky enough to catch our son's first comprehensible word too, but this one caused her more disappointment than it did to me. If I were to remind her about that even today, I'd get a prompt 'Fuck off' from my usually civil wife. Shlok's first word was 'Papa'!

Guessing Games

One does feel, a deep sense of elation,
When one makes out what a child says,
Decoding kids' tongue, deserves an ovation,
The happiness, and news, last for days!

It was such an awesome phase while Shlok was a lisping toddler, mispronouncing words. He would learn a new word, utter it wrong, sending us all scurrying to try and understand what he means by what he says.

This ended up becoming a very interesting guessing game for us, our friends and relatives, and even their friends. Especially with songs. Shlok would watch a song on TV, and later sing the song in his own mispronounced version. We would try to guess which song he is singing, and then seek help from all over, to know which exact song he is singing. The hunt for one particular Bollywood song became such a rage that Reshma's sister had to engage her college friends to help us understand which song he was referring to.

These instances turned out to be huge contests, with people claiming bragging rights about being the first ones to decipher Shlok's language. Eventual discovery of the song he was singing often led to uproarious laughter, when people tried singing the song in Shlok's signature style.

It wasn't just songs, but names too. Shlok's calling himself as 'Tlot', his mother as 'Late-Ma', or me as 'We-Wait', was funny, but obvious enough. What took the cake was him mispronouncing names of celebrities.

Bollywood actor Saif Ali Khan was mispronounced as 'Sir-Fazed-Khan'. India's best-known playback singer, Lata Mangeshkar became 'Lather Mangeshkar'.

It led to a lot of frenzied laughter, when we learnt that when Shlok said 'Buddha Baap' (Hindi for Old Father), he actually meant the first name of the legendary Indian actor Amitabh Bachchan.

And the best one, as to this day Shlok's mom insists on pronouncing the name of her favourite Hollywood actor, Dwayne 'the Rock' Johnson, as Shlok's oft-mispronounced 'Deewane Johnson'. 'Deewane' means 'crazy' in Hindi!

Often, we would end up replacing normal words and song lyrics with Shlok's mispronounced version, and I am sure we ended up irritating those unaware of the backstory.

Reshma, while laughing along at the guessing games, often tried teaching him the correct pronunciation, spending hours repeating the words to him, hoping that he would follow her direction. Shlok, mischievously, always insisted on mispronouncing the words, leading to a frustrated Reshma.

"One day, he will grow out of these lisping days, and you'll end up missing the days he mispronounced words and the ensuing guessing games." Calming down my worked-up wife is a tough task.

I tried further, "The way he speaks, the cute child's lisp, how he holds our finger while walking, we'll miss all this when he grows up. When he gets older, he'll probably dislike being spoken to in baby talk. Today, his life revolves around us. In the future, it will be all about his friends, his education. Then his career will take precedence over us, and eventually his spouse and his kids. You and I, we'll be left yearning for his attention. Let's enjoy this time when we are getting to see his days of innocence, his days of lisping, mispronouncing. He still likes being cuddled; hugs and kisses are the order of the day. He'll abhor being treated like a baby in just a few years. Let's make the most of this beautiful phase of life with our son, to cherish for the rest of our lives."

I was promptly rewarded with a kiss, and a tight hug. Seeing his parents hug and kiss, Shlok came running wanting to be part of the family hug.

Children grow up so very quickly, even before their poor parents realise it. Cut to the present day: Shlok is almost eleven years old, and he cringes when Reshma insists that her favourite Hollywood star is 'Deewane Johnson'.

Homebound No More

Dad goes to his workplace, far away, to town,
Mom also needs to go to office, each day,
No time to miss them, Granny takes me, too, down,
More people to visit, and with them, play!

With her maternity leave about to end, time was running out for Reshma, to spend exclusively with Shlok. She was fortunate to have spent all her maternity leave after childbirth. Had she carried Shlok full term, she would have lost a couple of weeks of maternity leave. This is because Reshma officially began her maternity leave, coincidentally from a day prior to when Shlok chose to take birth. Also, that he happened to be born on a public holiday abutting a weekend, meant three more precious days for her.

I had, of course, availed all of the max seven-day paternity leave granted by my employers, and made the most of that time with Shlok. Furthermore, one of the little perks of my being a salesperson was that I could adjust my time accordingly if I needed to be around at hand.

Sadly for her, Reshma had no such convenience. She knew that once she'd resume office, she would be swallowed full time into her desk-bound job, which often meant longer working hours.

A couple of weeks prior to resuming her office, she began sinking into deep despair over the eventuality of being unable to devote all her attention to her son. Her career, of course, remained important to her. Such is the dilemma that mothers the world over have to contend with, torn between their duties as a mother, and those of being a part of the workforce.

Nuclear families don't have the luxury offered by the large joint-family structure, where parents could leave their children in the care of other family members. We realised how important it is to have a support system around you, only after we became parents.

Shlok was, of course, in good hands. My mom had put in her papers at the large private hospital where she was stationed as a social worker, as soon as Shlok was born. She assured us that she would help take care of her grandchild till as long as it takes. Seasoned at child-rearing, my mom had given an exemplary upbringing to three of her own kids, as well as around five of our cousins. In fact, my cousins were all accustomed to addressing her as Mummy, much to her embarrassment. Imagine a woman being called Mummy by all eight kids in tow!

Come the day of Reshma's office resumption, she had made elaborate plans to leave for office before Shlok woke up, so he doesn't have to bear the ignominy of seeing his mother leave him and go. I, sensing that there will be a huge flood of emotions at home, left for office even earlier than usual.

That day, Shlok too, chose to wake up much earlier than usual. Reshma sent prayers to the heavens that her son does not throw a tantrum seeing her leave, nor insist on being taken along.

She got ready to leave for her office, requesting my mom to divert Shlok's attention while Reshma sneaked out. My firebrand mom, insisting that Reshma was doing nothing wrong by choosing to resume her work, encouraged her to be brave and wish a good day to her son, with a smile. She promised Shlok would reciprocate.

With tears streaming down her eyes, while standing at the door, Reshma mustered up a forced smile, waving to her darling son. Her morning prayers were granted, because Shlok kept up his side of the bargain. In my mom's arms, he waved back to Reshma, gestured a flying kiss, while he said a cute "Bye" with a warm smile. Then, he held the door, and swung it, closing the door.

Reshma was left crying inconsolably at the door, and kept weeping all the way to her office. Thankfully, I missed having to see all this emotional drama, else I'd have joined Reshma in her sobbing.

On one hand, she was happy to see her son cheerfully waving goodbye. She was assured he wouldn't miss her, and being taken care of by the safest hands possible. Hence, she was also confident she could resume her office. However, on the other hand, the mom in her was understandably forlorn. Feeling guilty for leaving her son behind while chasing her career aspirations, and I think secretly also a bit shocked, by his unceremonious goodbye. Mothers!

A few months later when Reshma had acclimatised to life as a full-time working mother, I was tucking Shlok in for the night. He refused to sleep, saying, "I don't want to sleep. If I sleep it will become tomorrow!" Reshma laughed out loud upon hearing this, saying she felt exactly the same way about going to bed every Sunday night, with Monday morning blues looming large.

Shlok, meanwhile, kept becoming a more gregarious little toddler. Once he became adept at walking and could speak a smattering of comprehensible words, he could hardly be tied down at home. He always wanted to be up and about. My mom would take him downstairs to the temple, and he would revel in the adulation which was showered upon him by neighbours.

Tugging at a neighbour's sleeve, he once spoke in his toddler lisp, "I want to go see your home." Upon which the neighbour requested my mom, and she had to relent. That day, we only saw Shlok back home in the evening. Eventually, that became an almost daily occurrence.

His grandmother would bathe him, and take him to the temple, eventually having to hand him over to the next besotted neighbour. Shlok would stare at people till they met his gaze, then flash his cutest impish smile. Invariably they would be drawn into a conversation, and he would ask to be taken to their home.

There were strict instructions to the security guards to not allow him to step out of the compound, but we almost never knew which of the 144 apartments within our housing society Shlok would be in, till he was delivered back home to us. Characteristically, while with one particular neighbour, he would meet another neighbour, and convince them into taking him along to their home as well. Be it an older child, man or woman, Shlok had a trick to turn on the charm offensive on any and all of them.

Mom, of course, kept tabs on his movement over the society intercom, but heaved a sigh of relief only when he came back smiling, fed on sweets and chocolates everywhere he went.

She once commented, "The way he badgers people into taking him along to their home, they might think that we starve him here at our place, and probably beat him up all day!"

Gravity Sucks

When it fell on his head, the apple, red mound,
Newton probably said, "Aw, shucks",
Else we'd all be floating and flying around,
If not for gravity, coz it really sucks!

In addition to gallivanting at our neighbours' apartments, Shlok loved being outdoors. Not that he complained if made to stay cooped up at home, but his preference was always to step out. Hence, my mom regularly took him to a playground in the late afternoons.

As with all children, Shlok loved the swing. He liked the slides too, but didn't really like the effort it took to climb up the stairs. Unless someone lifted him and placed him at the top of the slide, he didn't care too much for it. Same with the see-saw, as it took effort to push away from the ground. For an outdoorsy kind of little boy, he did behave pretty lazy. He was hence partial to the swing. This is because he would just need to hold the ropes and sit pretty while my mom did the heavy pushing.

He totally loved the breeze in his face and hair, and always insisted that Mom push the swing higher, and faster. Not a spring chicken anymore, Mom would eventually get tired. Other kids around often volunteered to push the swing while Mom caught her breath. They would venture pushing the swing faster and higher, much to Shlok's delight, and he'd jubilate with laughter.

One evening, while I was in a meeting at the office, my cell phone rang. Seeing that the caller was my mother, I excused myself from the meeting and stepped out.

"C-can you come home?" Mom sounded as if in tears, "Shlok was on the swing, and I was tired, so I sat on the bench. I asked another little child to push his swing, and it went too high, and fast, and... and..." She trailed off, crying and couldn't speak anymore.

Fearing the worst, I left office, and called my wife immediately, but couldn't get through to her. She sent me a message: Yes I know, rushing home.

We reached home at around the same time. Entering home, we saw our three-year-old son calmly asleep. Nothing seemed amiss, except that his chin was covered with a huge piece of cotton and gauze. Mom was pacing around, and upon seeing us come in, hugged us both and bawled her heart out. We calmed her down, then asked her what transpired.

"He was enjoying sitting on the swing, while that other boy pushed his swing faster and higher. I was seated on the bench right next to the swing. He was laughing, we were all smiling. Suddenly Shlok lost his grip on the ropes, and he fell. He fell from the top of the arc. On the ground. He hurt his chin badly. I am feeling so guilty. I should never have allowed him to... what have I done?"

Reshma took charge, "It is not your fault, Mummy. I'll check right away if the paediatrician is available later this evening."

"No, take him to the hospital, to the A&E. I mean, the Accident and Emergency unit. He's hurt his chin so bad, it was bleeding, so I applied some first aid. Still."

I jumped in, "Mummy, you have three sons of your own. You've raised eight kids. And managed countless family emergencies without batting an eyelid. Whoa, you've worked in a hospital! Why are you panicking so much?"

"But that's different. He is so small. Shlok. He's only three. I should have caught him but he..."

We left for the hospital immediately at my mom's insistence, while she elected to stay back so as not to make a crowd. Once in the cab, I saw tears rolling down Reshma's cheeks. She was badly shaken. I was panicking somewhat too, but couldn't express that in front of Mom or Reshma. We weren't aware of the extent of Shlok's injury, because Mom had dressed up the wound well. Reshma texted her youngest sister, who is a doctor, to meet us at the hospital.

The A&E doctor patiently told us that the dressing looked professionally done, and we should have let the same doctor treat Shlok, instead of rushing to the A&E. He said that while the wound was not deep, he would apply a couple of stitches for 'cosmetic reasons', saying the stitches would be removed in a week. "Don't worry, your son will survive!" he smirked.

On our drive back home, my sister-in-law broke the silence. "What is wrong with you guys? There was no reason for you to rush him to a hospital. Yes, one must be careful about injuries, and as lay people you understandably don't gauge the severity. Pardon my rage, but you idiots have run to the doctor even for his sniffles and scrapes. What can be solved with plain salted water and Dettol, makes you people seek medical professionals."

"When Shlok takes even a tumble, you guys make it national news. If he sneezes, you call in the cavalry. You even cry rivers when he gets his booster shots. I find it all so silly. I would suggest that the next time he has a fall, just rub some dirt on it and ask him to keep on playing. How will your son grow, when you as parents refuse to grow up?"

The message hit home. And hard. To be berated by your sister, nine years your junior, is quite an experience. We changed. And how! Let me give you a couple of examples, by jumping into the future again.

One day, a good Samaritan called up Reshma, saying her son has fallen down in the playground downstairs and is bleeding profusely. In office, she calmly called me, knowing that I was working from home that day, and asked me to go and check.

I changed quickly, went to the playground, saw nine-year-old Shlok lying on the condominium sidewalk, blood flowing down his thigh, and a little crowd surrounding him. I dispersed the crowd with, "You called me for such a small little thing? It's nothing, really."

I asked Shlok whether he could stand up, and then helped him walk back home. Cleaning up his wound with

Savlon, I switched on the TV for him, and he was a happy camper. Later that night we took him to a GP to dress up the wound properly.

I am not suggesting, in any way, that parents should adopt a cavalier attitude towards their children's health, but just to take a deep breath and not panic.

On another occasion, Reshma received a call from the school's nurse, informing her that Shlok had a nasty fall. Apparently, our ten-year-old son tripped while playing in the school playground, and fell backwards onto the roots of a tree, hurting his right hand. Reshma called me, informing me about the fall, assuring me that I needn't leave the office as she was already on the way to school. She'd keep me posted all through, of course.

She took Shlok to the GP, who suspected a fracture on his right wrist. They got an X-ray done, then went home, while the report was awaited. I reached home to see Shlok clutching his bandaged wrist, but smiling. I predicted that the X-ray report will surely be negative for any fractures, as someone with a broken arm can hardly afford to smile.

My son was affronted by my comment. "Papa, just because I am not crying my eyes out, doesn't mean that I am not in pain. It's just that I see no point in crying. If you really want to see how much I am in pain, here you go." He let out such a heartrending cry, that it made me realise I was wrong, and had underestimated the severity of his injury.

Sure enough, the reports indicated a hairline fracture on the wrist. We took him to the A&E, this time justifiably so, and got his arm plastered. He chose the colour of the plaster. Shlok spent the next couple of months being fawned over by his parents, teachers and friends.

That night, when we came back from the A&E, Reshma and I both shed tears seeing our son in pain.

She cried, "Why does my poor baby keep falling down so often?"

"Gravity, darling," I replied, "Gravity."

"I hate gravity. Gravity sucks."

Disaster Zone

Was it hit by an earthquake,
Or struck by a twister, a hurricane?
It's just a room messy, I take,
My little son, playing, it seems to explain.

We'd enrolled Shlok, at three years old, into a playgroup cum preschool, to help orient him towards a school setting, and also help expose him to children his age. Shlok, being the youngest in all our families and neighbourhood, was exceptionally pampered by all, so we wanted him to feel less special. Essentially not be treated like a celebrity. We also wanted him to make friends and get along well with the other kids.

On weekdays, a school van came to pick him up in the morning, and drop him back in the afternoon, along with other kids in the vicinity. Within the first week, the van staff (driver, cleaner, and van conductor) realised that Shlok is not a morning person.

Each morning, the bus conductor called out to Shlok while the van rolled into our apartment building, "Shlok, do you know, today they are going to play music in the school?"

That prospect, of music being played at the school, would invariably perk up sleepy Shlok's interest, and he'd readily agree to accompany them, waving out an enthusiastic goodbye to my mom. When I heard about this, I failed to see how he fell for the same ruse every which time.

Upon reaching the preschool, Shlok would instantly perk up to his usual friendly self, as was told to my mom by his teacher once. Apparently, he'd engage crying children by singing songs and cracking jokes, eventually making them smile.

It had been a couple of months since he'd joined the preschool, and I was curious to know how he spends his time at school. So I asked him how his day went. He said it was nice. I probed further, about what exactly he does in school, and what the teachers tell him.

He replied, "The teacher says, 'kiss my cheek, muah'. Then another teacher says, 'kiss my cheek too, muah'. They like me!"

I gave a bewildered expression to my wife, who laughed out loud when I said that I wished they had such schools when I was younger. Seeing his parents laugh, Shlok too joined in the laughter with glee.

A few weeks later, the preschool organised a parent-teacher conference. I felt a bit out of place as the hall was filled with only moms, and I could hardly see another father in attendance. I quit complaining when Reshma gently reminded me of my 'inclusive parenting' oath.

The teacher explained to us that in addition to social engagement, they were helping the children hone their hand-eye coordination. I raised my hand, and requested her to elaborate on the activities which helped children's hand-eye coordination. I was expecting to receive a response that the children play sports, and was already readying myself for an approving nod.

The straight-faced answer caught me off-guard, "We teach them paper tearing."

I could see other parents nodding but I could not resist blurting out, "Now I know why all my newspapers end up torn, despite us not having a dog at home!" Reshma was digging her elbow in my ribs, but I could hardly contain my loud chortling.

Given just a bag of toys, and a stack of newspapers, Shlok was capable of making a tidy living room look like it had been hit by a natural disaster, in a matter of minutes.

Once visiting my brothers' house, Shlok was sitting on the floor, playing with some miniature cartoon character toys kept atop a shelf, on the base of the TV unit. Panda is in the animation industry and uses these miniatures as models, then keeps them as memorabilia. We heard a loud crash, and suddenly saw Shlok rush away into the kitchen, to my mother. He'd apparently tapped the glass shelf with a toy, leading to it cracking. It looked like the glass shelf had been blown to smithereens, glass pieces and toys on the floor as if an earthquake had occurred.

Both my brothers readily pardoned their nephew, with Buzz actually marvelling at his miraculously unscathed escape. Panda has always been tolerant of Shlok's excesses. Shlok often calls my 6'3" tall, burly brother as his 'favourite toy'.

When I asked his indulgent uncles what they would have done if it were me who'd caused the damage, they replied matter-of-factly, "Difference between Shlok and you is that he is lovable. You, we'd have killed."

People told us it was because he is an only child, hence pampered and disorderly. But I've heard similar (or worse) horror stories from parents having two or even more children. Someone else told us that male children are more disordered, and daughters are ostensibly angels.

I can't blame this quality of his on Reshma, she has always shown signs of having mild OCD with her 'a place for everything, everything in place' rule. Probably it's me, then. Just like my favourite villain, the Joker, from The Dark Knight, I have always maintained that we thrive on chaos. But only till as long as I don't need to clean up after it.

Allow me to jump to the present day, briefly. Shlok is now ten years old. Recently, Shlok's homeroom teacher quipped, "Everything else about him is really almost perfect. If only I could teach him how to keep his desk in order, I'd be happier."

I smiled politely.

"Is he like this at home too?" he asked.

I could only respond with a sheepish, "Let's just say Shlok does not subscribe to a clean desk policy."

Shlok's probably going to hate me for writing this: My beloved child is living proof of the second law of thermodynamics, which says that entropy (or disorder) in an isolated system increases over time. Parents know this law better as: If you leave children unattended in a neat, clean room, you will find it wrecked in an hour.

Life is a Song

You can't mute it, change channels, or add,
I suggest you hum, or sing along,
Coz at times, it's crazy, it's happy, or sad,
But life is always, just singing a song.

Another one of Shlok's traits which could probably be ascribed to me is his constant humming of songs. Any given point in the day, if Shlok is awake, he'll be humming a song quietly, when not singing it aloud. Loud, screamingly loud.

Music appeals to all living beings, eliciting differing responses from everyone. Music is indeed a global language, it is also loved and appreciated by kids and grownups alike. Children take an instant liking to a rhythm.

I know about a colleague's child who refuses to sleep until she hears a lullaby sung by her mother. Which means, even if the mother is on a business trip, she is mandated to call at the scheduled sleeping time (in the time zone her child is), and sing a lullaby to her offspring. I found this amusing, and suggested to the mother that she could leave recordings of all her lullabies with her daughter the next time she is travelling on business. My suggestion was met with an angry glare. A mother's angry glare. I refrained from any further dialogue on this subject.

I am not claiming that all of Shlok's love for music comes from me. His mother also has a keen ear for rhythm, dances like a dream (to me), and has a taste for listening to good music. Listening to music, but not singing songs aloud every waking moment. My mom says I was exactly like that. Singing songs, uninhibited, all of the time, until asked to STFU. I've caught myself humming songs even at funerals.

My singing was limited to Bollywood songs, though. Not so with Shlok, as he would sing anything he had recently heard. Even advertisement jingles. Especially advertisement jingles. We always joked that Shlok only likes to watch TV for the ads, and has a future in the advertisement industry. He'd be disinterested in the TV programmes themselves, but come a commercial break and his ears would perk up to try and catch the jingle.

One particular incident comes to mind. Shlok had 'graduated' from his preschool (which also had kindergarten) and joined a primary school, at around five years of age. One day while on the school bus, en route to his school, he had apparently been listening to Hindi songs on the bus radio. His homeroom teacher was aghast to be greeted with a racy Bollywood number, "Touch me touch me, kiss me kiss me."

Thankfully, I didn't hear about this as a complaint from the teacher, but as a gleeful story related by the bus attendant. Shlok's class teacher must have probably thought that we fed a staple diet of B-grade films to our five-year-old boy.

I admit. I relive that part of my childhood when I see my son. He sings almost all the time. Yes, even when in the bathroom. The neighbours don't complain. They would, though, if I were to sing aloud.

When Shlok was around seven years old, I got an overseas opportunity from my employer. Reshma, happy for my career growth, welcomed the prospect of moving to Singapore, sounding pretty excited. She also assured me that she would be able to find a position in Singapore with her employer, an Indian MNC.

However, she was very apprehensive about how the move would affect Shlok. In India, we had a strong support system, our families, who would always look out for him, and us. Outside of our comfort zone, we'd be rendered alone in bringing up our son. Moreover, she was concerned about how he would adapt to a new country, new culture, new languages and a new school.

To quell the latter part of my wife's fears, I requested advice from the principal of my alma mater, who is also an active regional education advisor. We set up an elaborate conference call, to seek her counsel on what kind of school she recommended. She was pretty straightforward in her advice.

"Reshma, child, you mustn't worry about how Shlok would adjust, but about how you both as his parents would adjust. My request would be to not transfer your fears to the little child. He's all of seven. He will adapt in the blink of an eye. It is you guys I am getting worried about, as you are over-analysing."

"Children, they see change almost every day. Their bodies are always growing, their surroundings are changing. They see something new, never encountered before, almost every day. It is us as grownups who tend to get accustomed to our living atmosphere. For kids, life is like a song. There are some high notes, and some low notes. There are lilting cadences, varying rhythms, differing metre and tempo. An ever-changing, but a beautiful song. It is us adults who look at life as a series of crests and troughs of opportunities and threats."

"Trust me, he will adapt to life in Singapore better than you. He'll learn the new languages quickly, like he learns songs. I won't be worried about him even if you put him in a school where the medium of instruction is Japanese. It is you, as parents, who need to learn to appreciate change, and not worry too much!"

These words of wisdom held us in good stead as we embarked on the life-changing move to Singapore. We saw how Shlok took to life in Singapore like a fish to water, and we drew comfort from that.

In Singapore, I noticed that Shlok's daily singing routine continued. The choice of songs, however, underwent quite a sea change. He now mostly sings English numbers, is partial to rap, is eager to explore K Pop, but also adopts some of my kind of music. He still listens to Bollywood, and even sings along, while I run my playlist, invariably including those songs in his singing repertoire.

He's close to eleven years old now. His songs now are a veritable cultural cauldron of contemporary pop, retro rock, snappy rap, interspersed with potboiler Bollywood. Sometimes, even when he's singing at his loudest, I strain to make out what he is singing. Eminem (clean version, he clarifies) mostly, and other rap artists unbeknownst to me. I can hardly make out the lyrics he spouts out at an alarming speed. Suddenly Eminem gives way to a Bollywood number he recently picked up while watching Netflix, then quickly switches to Lennon's 'Imagine'!

However, on several occasions he breaks out into retro (for him, four years ago is retro) Bollywood, leaving me touched with a tear in my eyes, and a smile on my lips. My son is fast growing up from the pre-primary little kid he was in India, speaks with an un-Indian accent, but sometimes, just sometimes, gives me a glimpse of the younger Shlok when he breaks into "Touch me touch me, kiss me kiss me."

Singapore Beckons

My heart grows fonder,
I'll move there I reckon,
I want to go yonder,
Greener pastures, do beckon!

The move to Singapore was fun, but not bereft of some teething issues. In India, we had, in addition to the huge family support system, ample access to a small army of domestic help.

There was someone who would clean our car every morning. Dinner was taken care of by the cook. We had domestic help, and believe me, the help herself had a helper!

We are not royalty, all middle class families in India are accustomed to having these luxuries. Even today, when I ask Reshma what she misses most about India (except family, of course), she instantly replies, "My cook!"

This posed a challenge for Reshma. Having slobs for husband and son, with no domestic help, didn't help either. She eventually had to invoke her network of friends to find part-time cleaners.

The task of looking for a rented apartment was also arduous. All three of us had different 'asks'. I wanted an apartment nearby to our respective offices, with easy access to bus and metro. Reshma wanted to live close to the school we'd enrolled Shlok into. Seven-year-old Shlok was clear in his mind. He wanted to stay in a condominium where there was a big children's play area, and a huge swimming pool.

After the apartment was sorted, I once went to IKEA to buy some furniture, and had to lift and load so much of heavy stuff on my own. I was in disbelief when they said that they charge separately for delivery and assembly.

"How can they charge me for assembly?" I moaned to a colleague.

"What do you say assembly? Assembly is supposed to be something that you must D-I-Y, which stands for 'Do It Yourself', dude" he sniggered in response.

My son found it amusing too, "Papa, it would be so easy to follow the step-by-step instructions. Why would you need to pay to put the bed together? It looks just like Lego!"

"Where we come from, son," I replied, "if we need to change a light bulb, we call three people. First to change the bulb, second to hold the ladder, and the third one to turn the switch on and off!"

Evidently so, my son and I have differing reactions when a box says, 'some assembly required'.

The many conveniences which Singapore offered us far outnumbered these small issues.

In Mumbai, Reshma was used to monitoring every bit of Shlok's journey from home to school, school to day-care, day-care back to home. At every point of handover, she would obtain confirmations, similar to how you can track your packages with some courier company's website. All this, while working hard in her office.

In Singapore, we could draw comfort from the fact that it is amongst the safest places on earth. As parents, we felt comfortable in having Shlok walk to and from school by himself. This involved crossing major roads, but we knew we could trust drivers in Singapore to follow all traffic signals and rules. We'd also entrusted Shlok with a condominium access card and house keys. He didn't complain about having to stay alone till one of his parents reached home.

However, our son found one particular thing as an 'invasion of privacy'. A Singaporean friend had reminded us that 'low crime doesn't mean no crime', meaning we mustn't be too careless. Being concerned parents, we had installed a small CCTV camera in the living room, to assure us about Shlok being home, and safe. He often complained to his paternal grandmother, his maternal grandparents, and everyone who'd care to listen, that his parents were 'policing' over him by installing the camera.

Although he didn't mind letting himself in every day to an empty home, he would get somewhat uncomfortable when it got a bit dark. Reshma and I tried so that one of us reached home before sundown. However, on the days we got a bit late, we'd enter to see all lights in each corner of the house switched on, and the radio turned on at full volume.

I feel that this change has also contributed to making my son a bit more responsible and independent. One day I reached home to see Shlok munching into a sandwich. He saw me eyeing his food, and offered to make a sandwich for me.

I couldn't believe my ears when my seven-year-old son asked me what seasoning I would prefer on the sandwich. When I didn't respond, he spelt out my options: Oregano, Chili Flakes, or Italian herbs. Disbelief was writ large on my face as till just a few months back he was so used to being spoon-fed.

Yet to recover from the shock of being offered a sandwich with several choices, I was served a sumptuous-looking microwave-heated sandwich, molten cheese dripping out invitingly. There were potato chips as sides on the plate too.

I was unable to respond to this sarcastic comment with my mouth full of delicious food, "Enjoy your sandwich, Papa. I can now safely reheat and relish mine without the risk of you stealing my food."

Food for Thought

To love a toy, a pet, e'en dearer,
Is the love of a person, oh, so good,
But there is no love sincerer,
Than, of course, the love of food!

Ah, food. Food, for some people, is only a means of nourishment. For others, it's an emotional topic. No half measures with Shlok. For him, food is an obsession. In this chapter, I'll take you on a whirlwind trip of incidents involving my son, and his decade of love-hate relationship with food.

Reshma misses his infant days a lot, when she would introduce a variety of solid foods to our little one, and he in turn uncomplainingly swallowed it all up. As he grew up, he became increasingly choosy and fussy about what he eats.

I remember once coaxing a toddler Shlok into eating a banana. He took one small bite, then pointing at the fruit gestured as if asking what it was called. I tried teaching the name of my favourite fruit to my son. "Banana, this is called Banana." Shaking his head, he declined my offer of another bite with both his answer, and a new name for this tropical fruit, "Na, Na". Now ten years old, Shlok cringes at even the mention of eating a banana, though he plays a video game called 'My Friend Pedro', where the protagonist is led into violence by a Banana.

Offered a potato though, Shlok can devour it by the bucketful. Potato chips, French fries, wedges, Indian samosas or vadas, potato patties in burgers, mashed potatoes, Swiss Rosti. All of these dishes involving the versatile potato find equal favour with Shlok.

"What's for food" is not a question from Shlok, but often meant as a challenge to Reshma. He hates being served the same dish more than once a week.

"Momsie," he goes, "Papa likes eating the gruel you make and won't complain if you serve it up 365 days a year. For me, can you please cook something nice and spicy?"

He prefers monotony broken by different tastes on his palate, across all cuisines, as long as the ingredients don't include his dislikes. Both my mother and my mother-in-law welcome his challenges with enthusiasm, and he in turn rewards them with the plates wiped and fingers licked clean.

Shlok isn't fussy about cuisine, as long as what is served to him is vegetarian. Reshma ascribes his distaste of non-vegetarian food to a probable past birth as an Indian saint, while I suspect that my devoutly vegetarian mother's upbringing is deeply ingrained in Shlok's food preferences.

Travel, to most of us, is about the sights and sounds, and touristy landmarks. For Shlok, it is the food on offer. He's as much at home in an upmarket restaurant in Europe, as while eating street food in the bylanes of Mumbai. He loves the spicy explosion of taste lent by street food across India, but he also adores the assault by Mexican food on his tingling taste-buds. He had begged with us to order another wrap at a Falafel-land outlet in Santorini. I had to literally drag both him and Reshma out of the Lindt store in Paris.

Our move to Singapore offered him access to global cuisine, with a plethora of food options available from across the world.

He is partial towards Italian fare though. Pizza and pasta are his comfort food. He simply loves cheese. His love for cheese, of all kinds, shows. He reminds me that paneer, which is his favourite Indian food ingredient, is also cheese, cottage cheese.

"You must introduce your son to some healthy and nutritious food. If he only gorges on potato and cheese, he will continue to be fat and unhealthy. Also, please push him to work out, or take up a sport. He is, what, ten now? Really needs to build a better shape." My fit and health-freak friend cautioned me.

I replied, "Yeah, I agree with you wholeheartedly. But I just cannot push him beyond a point. Unless he himself feels deeply about losing his baby fat and flab, anything I say will fall on deaf ears."

"So will he always overeat, always be fat, and remain unhealthy? There are a so many pitfalls associated with being fat. Diabetes and heart issues run in both yours and Reshma's families. Also, nobody runs in your families!"

"Lame joke, bro. But I expect this fat stuff to last only till the first heartbreak," I assured, "because the day he realises he needs to be in decent shape, to win the attention of the girl he wants to make a girlfriend, the drive for a six pack will come. He will have to then decide between cheese and cheesy lines, and choose between sweet dumplings and sweet nothings."

For all his liking for food, Shlok still has no love lost for fruits. I had once overheard a telephonic conversation between Reshma and him.

"Shlok, I've kept grapes in the fridge. Please eat them. I expect to see the grapes finished when I'm home this evening."

"But Mumma, our ancestors ate grapes only because they didn't get to eat nachos with an avocado dip!"

Knowing Shlok's distaste for fruits, yet wanting him to ingest some nutritious fruits, Reshma thought of buying a juicer. I am too ill-informed to know the distinctions between blender, juicer and food processor, so let's please stick with 'juicer'.

Each evening, after returning from office, Reshma would whip up a juice or smoothie, and ask us to guess the ingredients. Shlok was around nine then. Initially we would sportingly compete to guess the ingredients. I would invariably fail.

My excuse? Moving to Singapore had exposed Shlok to so many international fruits, compared to the indigenous fruits I ate in my childhood. So it was easy for him to identify the exotic fruits that Reshma would add to the mixed fruit juice, while I was left guessing.

The enthusiasm though, waned after a few weeks. Ours, not Reshma's. She continued to search for interesting fruit combinations, and to challenge us to guess what went into her innovative concoctions.

One day, she'd gone pretty adventurous with her experiments. First sip in and Shlok made a face. Exactly the same face he'd made when he'd first tasted a lemon as a toddler. Being a dutiful husband to my beautiful wife, I gulped the 'juice' without protesting. I needed to be a good role model to my son, didn't I?

As usual, Reshma asked us to guess the ingredients, "So, who can tell me what fruits I've made this juice with?" Shlok's hand went up instantly, and Reshma eagerly awaited his answer. His answer made me erupt in laughter, and Reshma in anger.

While we were still served juices after that, it was the last ever episode of 'Guess the fruits in the juice' contest at our home.

Shlok, with mock enthusiasm, said, "I've played this game ever since you bought that juicer. I am really sorry about this one. I don't know the other ingredients, Mumma, but one thing is for sure. You've made this thing with shit. That's exactly what this juice tastes like!"

Muahahaha

It takes lots of hard work, this new world and struggle,
To get out of my comfort zone,
Yes, I may get kind words, and love and snuggle,
But to grow up I must do it alone.

To imply that our move from Mumbai to Singapore was seamless, would be an error on my part. The three of us were seasoned travellers even before the opportunity to move to Singapore presented itself. However, going to a foreign country as a tourist, versus moving there, are concepts worlds apart.

Singapore, indeed, has a 'plug and play' convenience in settling in, but we had our own personal challenges to deal with.

Reshma had to invoke all her accumulated leaves, to ensure a smooth transition for both Shlok and me. She also shuttled twice between India and Singapore to organise the movers' shipment of the stuff we wanted to send across to Singapore.

At seven years old, Shlok had been enrolled into grade three at the school. Being the protective mother she is, Reshma also accompanied Shlok to his school the first few days, while also getting involved in the PTA at school, in order to create a school support group.

I was myself struggling with the change of scene, and managers' differing professional expectations from me, so I could hardly contribute to helping Shlok acclimatise to the new environment. All I could do was to give him, and myself, the motivational mantra, that 'the more things change, the more they remain the same', and that we must rely on the constants in life to help contend with the variables.

There is no denying the fact that Shlok and I took more than ten days to adjust to the small 2.5 hours' time difference between India and Singapore. Over the years of leisure travelling, I've discovered that while Shlok and I find it very difficult to manage our circadian rhythm, Reshma can comparatively quickly overcome jet lag.

A few months into the school year, Reshma attended a meeting requested by Shlok's homeroom teacher. When she came back from the meeting, I could sense that Reshma was visibly shaken, but she said she'd speak with me when Shlok was not within earshot.

His homeroom teacher had told Reshma that she had been observing Shlok for a few months now, and became increasingly concerned with his verbal pauses, and consistent stuttering. She recommended consulting a speech therapist to help with our son's perceptible speech impairment. Shlok had always seemed slow in forming sentences, but we always ascribed that to careful selection of appropriate words by a nimble brain, rather than it being an outright disability. We were petrified, to say the least.

I told Reshma that while the teacher's observations were well-intentioned, she has known Shlok only since a few months, whereas we have known him for all of his life. My wife's response was logical too. She said that while we have known only one child, ours, the teacher has several years of experience of managing and educating innumerable children.

We also consulted Shlok's now-favourite teacher in school, his instructor in French, who was always appreciative of his quick adoption of a language hitherto unheard by him, and never by his family. She heard us out, and suggested that since the homeroom teacher sees more of Shlok, she might mostly be correct in her observation. However, she hazarded a guess to something altogether different.

Coming from Mumbai, where his family and friends mostly conversed in Hindi, it meant that Shlok thinks in Hindi, she explained to us. Translation of Hindi to English while speaking is something almost every Indian has to learn. Compounded with the fact that now Shlok had to unlearn his Indian accent of speaking English, and adapt to speaking in a manner more discernible to his peers and teachers, meant an added effort for him. She assured us that there is nothing wrong with the Indian accent, but in order to be accepted by his friends, Shlok was putting in the extra effort to speak in their accent. She thought that this might also be a factor accentuating his stammer.

I didn't dare to tell her that I'd been guiding Shlok against taking on a fake accent which doesn't come naturally to him. My kid was, but naturally, confused.

Acknowledging the issue at hand, my wife and I undertook a mission, to try and see if we could help Shlok, keeping speech therapy as a last alternative. I have to mention here that there is probably no scientific basis to what we did, but parenting, as we've realised, is a lot of trial and error.

First, we tried intervention, albeit differently. In a conversation, when we saw our son stuttering, we'd interject, reminding him that he stuttered, and encouraged him to start over again. This made him see that stuttering wouldn't help him to communicate, and we were hoping that if intermittent stuttering were a habit he'd picked up, this would help him do away with it.

The second tactic was easier. Shlok had always been a big fan of a few YouTubers. He had, on several occasions, mentioned to us that he wanted to become a professional YouTuber. Seeing my revulsion towards one of his favourite YouTuber, whom I jokingly called 'a peacock-haired joker', my son had since stopped mentioning YouTube vlogging as a career option for himself.

We encouraged Shlok to create a YouTube channel, and promised to be his first subscribers. Emboldened by his parents' support, he uploaded a couple of videos. We invited our friends and family to subscribe to the channel as well. Shlok was ecstatic, but we were happier. His videos had zero stuttering, which meant we had stumbled upon something right, in our endeavour to help him.

Reshma sent the videos to his homeroom teacher, who welcomed the videos; and also the seamless speech from Shlok, which she never saw while in her class. However, she cautioned us that speaking to a camera is different to social settings where Shlok still continued to stutter.

This led to us invoking our third tactic, which came by as a coincidence. The dramatics teacher in Shlok's school was looking for some children for her annual Christmas play, with that year's edition involving actors portraying characters from various festivals around the globe.

Shlok has always been fond of dramatics. Even as a toddler, I often caught him practising different expressions looking into a mirror. So, drawing his interest, we suggested that he try auditioning for a role. He expressed curiosity in a naughty character (Jack O'Lantern) in the play. I helped him perfect the evil laughter needed for the role, 'Muahahahaha!'

Shlok bagged the role, and was very happy, as it helped him make a lot of new friends, also earning him some necessary 'cred'. He worked hard to learn his lines, with Reshma and I helping him with his cues by playing other characters in his home practice sessions. It was hard work for him, but a lot of fun for us as a family.

Come showtime, Shlok put in a stellar performance. His cute, innocent, naughty expressions won all hearts. His dialogue delivery was flawless. Reshma and I were in endless applause, crying and smiling all through the show. The only two people in that auditorium clapping harder for him were: Shlok's homeroom teacher and his French teacher.

All the World's a Stage

I was a lisping child yesterday,
But today life has turned a page,
They stand and applaud when I say,
Confidently, "All the world's a stage!"

The French teacher caught up with us, congratulating us with hugs on our involvement in helping Shlok put in a faultless performance. She informed us that she collaborates with the dramatics teacher for an annual performance involving William Shakespeare's plays.

Children in grades 4-6, aged 9 through 11 perform roles in these plays, and she said that she would want Shlok to participate in the next year's event, by when Shlok would be nine-ish. As a primer for us, she invited us to that year's event. We, of course, eagerly accepted.

The performance we attended was in a larger theatre, and ran a full house. The play was based on Shakespeare's play, 'The Tempest', which we barely remembered reading during our younger days.

We were astonished to see the barely pre-teen actors on the stage, exuding confidence while spouting long, really long lines in what we call 'Shakespearean English'.

I could hardly make out a word of what they said, yet pretended to get it and nodded at the ongoings on the stage. Reshma was less subtle, when she said, "Hey can you make out what these kiddos are saying? I can't understand a word!" I was less embarrassed with what she said aloud than with what Shlok was doing. The fat critter had fallen asleep and was snoring loudly!

We slinked out of the auditorium, hoping to leave unnoticed, and fervently hoping that the good teacher forgets all about casting Shlok in the following year's programme.

She remembered, and insisted that we sign him up when the auditions opened the next year. The play selected for that year's performance was Shakespeare's 'Macbeth'. I would have been satisfied even if Shlok had got a bit part in such a huge cast, but my son had lofty goals. He auditioned for, and landed, the role of King Duncan.

No, I was not aware of the significance of the role till I read the script. The script was an enormous book, where Shlok's part included longish lines, and I could make neither heads nor tails of what the lines meant. My convent-educated wife, too, found the script Greek and Latin. Else she'd have roasted me to no end. Phew!

Shlok had realised that being cast as King Duncan was a huge opportunity for him, and understood that we'd be unable to help him this time around. So he took it upon himself to put in extra efforts, and ended up understanding and memorising not only his own lines, but the entire script.

I believe that participating in that play helped Shlok become more mature and responsible. It also helped him get acquainted with older children, and lent further gravitas to his reputation within the school campus.

The performance included musical renditions within the play, with songs composed by the music teacher and the students themselves. One of the songs was based on a line from Shakespeare's comedy 'As You Like It'. The song was titled: 'All the world's a stage'.

I could not find a single performer fumbling a note, or missing any cue. Of course, this time we went much better prepared, carefully poring over the script, humming the song lyrics.

As a parent, it seemed to me that my little child had metamorphosed into this confident actor, delivering his lines like a seasoned thespian.

Shlok went on to portray the titular character in the following year's performance based on Shakespeare's 'Julius Caesar'. The trio of his dramatics teacher, music teacher and French teacher all unanimously lauded his commitment and undying enthusiasm throughout the rehearsals.

We were all made to sign an undertaking, with Shlok mandated to give up his lunch recess for rehearsals. We had to agree to not plan travel around key dates for the rehearsals and performances. My wife went through pretty gruelling logistics exercises, picking up and dropping our son to and from school, and racing to and from the airport as some of our trips were already planned and couldn't be rescheduled.

Shlok ended up skipping watching movies on these flights, choosing to read his lines instead.

When asked how he managed to memorise his lines, especially the long monologues of Caesar, Shlok, by then ten years old, replied, "My dad himself couldn't understand any of the lines at all. His 'much-vaunted' English vocabulary and fluency were practically useless. So I doubled up my efforts. I memorised my lines on flights, in hotels, even when in the toilet."

Et tu, Brute!

Good Cop, Bad Cop

My mom gives me the loving words and look,
Intimidating ones are given by my Pop,
But I know it's the oldest trick in the book,
My parents play 'Good Cop, Bad Cop'!

Moving to Singapore meant we didn't have the everyday physical presence of our parents. Yes, video calls exist, but they don't really suffice.

Shlok had spent the first five to six years of his life under the aegis of my mom. We were, of course, around as parents, but Reshma and I could fool around with Shlok as my mother played the necessary role of overarching family elder. She would spoil Shlok crazy, but when required, her stern voice kept him (and me) from mischief.

In our efforts to expose Shlok to the global megacity that Singapore is, we didn't want him (or even us) to be lost in the glitz and glamour.

Reshma and I decided that one of us needs to be stern with him, while the other can be the friendly parent. We couldn't both afford to be stern with him, nor both allow him to have the run of the house. An additional logic I added was that Shlok, being the youngest in the entire clan, is the classic 'runt of the litter' and is pampered by all. One family member needed to be less lenient, and act as the balancing factor.

To her credit, my wife left the choice to me. I could choose to be the friendly father, with her taking the mantle of the manic mom. But I chose the other option, wanting to be the alpha male in the house, and get to throw my weight around.

As being stern doesn't come naturally to me, Reshma helped build a whole backstory of an angry dad with Shlok. She told our son that she defers to his Dad on all important (and not-so-important) matters, hence the proverbial buck in the family stops with his father.

Shlok, it seemed, had accepted the newly-laid family structure. So, everything from being allowed an extra scoop of ice cream to his access to screen time began to be governed by me.

It appeared, on the surface, that I was running the ongoings of our household with an iron fist. As any married man will testify, this is far from reality. The really important decisions, of course, are always made by the wife.

This happens all the time. Managing (controlling?) stuff in the background, while it appears to the observer, that I am the boss of the house unilaterally calling all the shots.

As an example, she'll tell me that Shlok should be eating healthy stuff, which leads to me insisting with him to eat fruits, declining his demand for a cheese pizza. I thunder, "Eat an apple instead, your mom has kept apples for you and asked me to cut and serve them to you."

Guess what happens when Shlok's mom returns from her office to see her son sitting glum? She whips up a cheese-filled sandwich for him. "You want more, my baby?"

My raised eyebrow is just waved off with, "It is fine, to indulge once in a while, he'll run it off in the playground."

"But darling, was it not just this morning when you asked me to desist from ordering pizza for him, and to make him eat those apples?"

Reshma just clicks her tongue, "Oh please don't be so grumpy, Daddy, I'll make delectable cheese sandwiches for you too."

That's exactly how the discussion ends. I have many more such instances, but I intend to write a book, and am not really looking for a divorce!

Guess who comes out smelling of roses, as a loving, caring, nurturing parent to Shlok? Shlok's Mom!

Guess who is the dour, sour-faced, foul-mood, evil, grumpy, villain in Shlok's life? Of course, Shlok's Dad!

Over time, I noticed Shlok was getting closer to his mother, telling her things which he wouldn't tell me. She'd come to know things first, then convey onward to me. Like his first crush. I'd envisaged my son will tell me about his first ever crush. But no, his mom got to learn about it before I did. I heard about it from her and not him.

Reshma could read that my being strict with our son was taking its toll on me. She would often say that she saw how not giving in to all of our loved son's childish demands, causes consternation to me. She often caught me crying alone after I'd been stern with him. Did she ever do anything about it? "But dear," she'd tease me, "you had asked to be the strict father, didn't you?"

It is indeed unbearably heart-wrenching, to punish someone whom you love to no end. But you really need to steel yourself to be strict in your behaviour towards the very person you are biologically programmed to love endlessly. I guess this is where parenthood differs between the mother approach and the father approach.

A mother is designed to unconditionally love and nourish her offspring all her life. A father, however, wants to prepare his child for a life without him.

I am man enough to admit a deep connection with my emotional side. I have no shame in admitting that it hurts me more than it hurts Shlok when I have to be firm with him. The dad in me is always in a state of dilemma between wanting to spoil Shlok crazy, and yet needing to keep such feelings in check. As a parent, I want to buy him all luxuries that I couldn't get as a child, but at the same time I want my son to be humble, be less materialistic, and be strong enough to face a hard life, if tides turn.

One day, in a weak moment, I admitted to my then eight-year-old son that I so hate being a strict dad, "But it is necessary for one parent to remain firm. The kid needs to be made to understand that not everything in life comes so easy, and we must appreciate the value of money."

I continued, "Today, I can understand my own father, and all the vilified fathers in the world. You do know, that as your father, for me you are my joy and pride, but also my biggest weakness." I kept on blabbering and was close to tears, when he raised a hand, wishing to speak.

"Hey, Dad, remember when I was four, we'd gone to Disneyland? There, I'd made us all wait in a long queue for three hours just so I could shake hands with Spiderman? I was such a huge fan of Spidey that I wore a Spiderman costume to watch my first Spiderman movie. I so wished for us to move to New York so I could see Spidey swing around the Big Apple, ha! Standing in front of Spiderman, I was so star-struck that I could barely say anything to him."

Wiping away a tear, I said, "Yeah, I had to do all the talking with the Spidey character because you got so tongue-tied and awe-struck breathing the same air as your favourite superhero! But, beyond nostalgia, what's your point here, Shlok?"

"My point is, even back then I kinda suspected that Spiderman isn't real, and the guy was just wearing a costume, playing his part. I'm now double that age, and at eight, I can see through the playacting."

He continued, "What you are doing is, just like Spidey, playing a part. Mumma is the good cop, and you're the bad cop. It's the oldest trick in the book, you know?"

My Oh Myopia

I keep rubbing my eyes, blurry,
I can't see anything distant, from afar,
I'll wear my glasses, no worry,
And it's the clearest I've seen, by far!

Parenting involves a lot of research. Along our journey on parenting, we, have done quite a lot of research on a number of topics.

One of the topics of our Google research was about the increasing phenomenon of Myopia, or short-sightedness (also called near-sightedness to appear less disparaging), in children across the globe. While various researchers estimate differing percentages of young children affected by myopia across geographical regions, they all more or less agree that the number of cases are increasing at alarming rates.

In several East Asian countries, it is estimated that myopia affects around 80-90% of high school students.

Apparently, the onset of myopia happens at around six to seven years of age (or less), and progresses on till mid-teens. At around fifteen to sixteen years of age, it stabilises.

Asian children are most prone to developing myopia, although I am not sure whether that has anything to do with the sheer number of children in Asia.

But why, in this midst of my tale about my roller-coaster experiences of fatherhood, did I add this balderdash? Well, it all circles back to my sweet little son.

Even as a toddler, Shlok would crane his neck, rub his eyes, and try to view things as up, close and personal as possible. The TV, people, food, toys. He could hardly keep a safe distance. We attributed this to his inquisitive nature.

In school, Shlok liked to be in the thick of things. He wanted to sit up front, and didn't like being in the third row of any school activity. Even during school excursions, he insisted on being close to the presenter/screen/action. We marvelled at our son's academic inclination at such an early age.

All of the aforementioned research described at the start of this chapter, was done on a post-facto basis.

We had discovered that in Singapore my employers' medical coverage didn't include anything to do with the eyes. Unless if there's an accident involved. That is not something we wanted to encounter in order to get our eyes checked.

In one of our frequent trips to Mumbai, the three of us went to an ophthalmologist for a routine eye checkup. I found it funny that my eight-year-old son couldn't make out the trees or the woods or whatever it was that his eye-test included. My test was mundane letters, but apparently they even make eye check-ups for kids entertaining.

The doctor, unfortunately, didn't find it funny at all. Shaking his head, he said that it is becoming eerily common for children to be diagnosed with myopia. He recommended corrective glasses for Shlok, and advised us that the 'number' will progress higher as Shlok grows older and taller.

My mother didn't take it well, at all. She was crying, inconsolably so, "My oh my, my little boy. My oh my, he has to wear spectacles at such a young age…"

My funny brother interjected, "Ma, it's not 'My oh My'. It's called 'My oh pia', 'Myopia'. Try again."

"Children these days, hardly go out to play. If their eyes are not accustomed to seeing things afar, the eyes get used to not seeing in the distance." This was a message from an uncle of Reshma. I couldn't find fault in this rationale, which continued with, "In our childhood, we were hardly found at home. Parents these days are so protective about their kids that they don't allow them to stay out for long. Children only stay indoors, and hence the eye muscles don't get enough exercise to see further away."

"You, you ass, this is all because of you," I threw shade at Panda, "you should never have gifted him the iPad. All he does the entire day is watch YouTube videos on that device. It was bound to spoil his eyes. You indulge him too much for his own good." I was so convinced my brother was to be blamed.

He simply gave me the finger and laughed, "Do you remember how he asked for the iPad though?"

Shlok was around four, when one day he asked my mom to place a call to Panda, who was back then stationed in Singapore. He asked her to tell Panda that he wanted a tablet. Shlok's grandmother was a bit confused, as to why he wanted a tablet, unaware of the new-gen lingo. Her grandson then explained that what he wanted was not the medicinal variety of tablet, but a Wi-Fi enabled electronic device, for him to play games on. Lo, the indulgent uncle of his carried back a new iPad for Shlok on his very next trip home.

"Probably this is hereditary." Reshma said to me in confidence. She'd read that a parent having myopia increases propensity of their child to have the same condition. She was bespectacled ever since I knew her in college. Her youngest sister too. My wife was afraid she'd passed on myopia to our son.

My mother-in-law also chimed in, "He doesn't eat any green leafy vegetables, that's a factor too. You guys must ensure he eats carrots. All he does is eat cheese and potatoes!" Yes, she said this while serving spoonfuls of her sumptuous cottage cheese preparation into our plates. Mothers!

"Shlok, you should do some exercise for your eyes too." Saying this, my mom taught Shlok some eye exercises to perform daily.

I had no idea which of these reasons were a factor causing Shlok's myopia. I was, till then, blessed with 20/20 natural vision, pushing thirty seven years of age. So I resolved to try all of these suggestions, upon our return to Singapore.

Meanwhile Shlok was busy selecting some cartoon-character frames, to impress his friends in Singapore.

When we were back in Singapore, one weekend my son and I were seated on the balcony in our apartment. "Papa, how come you have 20/20 vision?" Shlok asked me, "Uncle tells me you were a fat boy, lounging at home all day, eating buttered bread, when you were my age."

I snickered, "I grew up in a city which had amazingly beautiful girls. The city we are now living in, has equally, if not more beautiful, women from across the world."

This caught Reshma's attention. She has this weird ability to hear from miles away when I say something self-incriminating. Prodded to elaborate, I went on.

"Your favourite toy and my brother, Panda, often said that if the body is a temple, then we must pay obeisance to all beautiful bodies. I took that mantra to heart. My close friends did so too. We made it our daily business to admire all girls, all directions, all distances. Alternating between the girls closer to us and ones in the distance. We would watch them coming from afar, keep watching them till we see them disappear into the horizon. All of us friends, till today, don't have to wear any glasses. That, is owing to lots of eye exercise done during our teenage days, to last us a lifetime."

On a serious note, we had to put in major curbs on the screen time Shlok enjoyed. He had to say goodbye to his YouTube channel. I will elaborate on the measures we agreed upon in the forthcoming chapter, but we had to take some drastic steps to limit further deterioration of his eyes.

Once, I saw Shlok remove his newly-acquired glasses momentarily, then wear them again. Out of curiosity, I asked him what he feels about wearing spectacles.

With wide-eyed amazement, my bespectacled mini-me replied, "I always thought that the world was naturally blurry beyond a few feet, Papa. I never knew that things in the distance can appear so clear. Wow!"

The Screen Trials

Some of carrots, some ploys of stick,
Like a baby, being tried to wean,
My Dad, many strategies, did pick,
To keep me away from the screen.

In order to wean him away from his natural predilection towards screens (mobiles, iPad, computer, and TV), we had to take a few drastic measures.

The first step was, as always, the most impractical one. We asked Shlok to desist from watching anything on the screen beyond an allotted one hour a day. This became very difficult to monitor, with both Reshma and I working full-time. We didn't want to end up in an awkward situation where Shlok lied to us about accessing the screens, as that would inevitably lead to bigger lies.

The second strategy bombed too. A total ban on his screen time. He was disallowed from watching anything at all. This didn't go down well with him. Within a couple of days of introducing this new measure, when Reshma asked Shlok to run an errand, he flatly declined.

This is uncharacteristic of Shlok. He's as lazy as a sloth. (Come to think of it, Shlok and sloth almost rhyme if you lisp a bit!) He'll reason, or charm, his way out of hard labour, but never be rude. When Reshma asked him why not, Shlok's sullen response was, "I won't do it. I am a boy who has nothing to lose." Reshma understood that screen time was one of our leverages over him. She suggested a rethink on this strategy.

Our third idea was math. Like every kid ever (with few rare exceptions like Reshma), Shlok hated math. I hated math. My dad hated math. It is our family tradition then: to hate math.

In order to develop his math skills, Reshma enrolled him into math enrichment classes, outside of his schooling hours. They gave him loads of homework. Parents just love it when their kids are given a lot of homework. It keeps the critters occupied. So my next proposition to Shlok was: if he does one hour of his math enrichment homework, he gets an equitable hour of screen time.

I patted myself on the back for such a bright idea. Reshma approved it too. It worked like a charm for a few weeks. But Shlok was growing up, and had other ideas.

Whenever he wants to remind himself, or us, about something important, he writes it on a magnetic whiteboard we have placed on our fridge. In a few weeks since this new idea was put into practice, we saw written on the whiteboard:

'Mumma and Papa agree that Shlok will stop going to math class.'

Needless to say, my idea turned out to be a big dud. Reshma hated me for connecting his screen time allocation to his math class.

We were running out of ideas. Using a corporate analogy, we wanted to use 'carrot' strategies to incentivise Shlok, as opposed to 'stick' plans.

The solution to our predicament came about a few weeks later, in the form of a figurative knock on the door, or a ringing of the doorbell. A couple of the children from our condominium came calling for Shlok, asking if he would join them downstairs in the playground. Shlok politely declined, and went back into his room.

"Why not?" I asked. "Shlok, if you go downstairs, play for an hour, come back all red and sweaty, you get half an hour of screen time, what do you say?"

His eyes lit up, meaning I was onto something right. "So Papa, what if I play for two hours, then?"

That day onwards, we have continued this practice of associating Shlok's screen time as a factor of the time he spends playing outdoors. We keep tweaking the multiplier depending on the situation. Currently he gets an hour of screen time for each hour of playing.

The time he spends away from the screen, playing with his friends, makes him sociable, and hopefully also helps burns some of the fat he lugs around his waist.

I was very satisfied with this turn of events, and I popularised my successful idea with several of my friends and colleagues, who are also parents to young kids.

A few of them implemented similar models with their children, thanking me for the idea. One friend of mine wanted my help in designing a proposition for his son. I hope these parenting tips help their young ones avert myopia.

Another friend congratulated me for coming up with an innovative win-win solution. A classic case of killing two birds with one stone, he said. Sorry PETA. Maybe feeding two birds with one scone, then?

Think Out of the Idiot Box

Losing one form of entertainment,
Opened vistas for other things, with enthusiasm,
What was seen as mere punishment,
Helped him to cross, many an unknown chasm.

Curtailing Shlok's unrestricted access to screen time also resulted in extra bonuses, which I am convinced shall help him in his all-round development. By not having a screen to passively stare into, Shlok developed some other interests which didn't usually involve a screen.

First hobby he picked up was Origami. I was used to calling it 'craft'. He explained to me that it is the Japanese art of paper-folding. I helped encourage his interest in craft, by buying for him lots of origami paper. In a few weeks' time, we were overwhelmed with the clutter of paper planes, paper boats, origami cranes, origami balls, origami hearts and other such items all around the house.

Reshma threw his works of art in the bin, and I hid all the remaining unused origami paper. Doing that curtailed, somewhat, his experiments with origami. We still sometimes see an odd paper plane or two, using our living room as a makeshift hangar, but it is still manageable.

After losing his origami paper, he caught the bug of cryptology. He wanted to create a new cipher, and challenge his friends to crack the code. He announced his aspiration to become a cryptologist one day; to help create and decipher codes, save lives, and make millions. That passion was short-lived too.

Later, Shlok discovered that Singapore has a very efficient library network, and literally dragged me to a nearby library to sign him up as a member. Impressed with the range of reads they offered, I promptly took membership. Truth be told, Shlok helped me rediscover my own childhood love for reading.

Soon, our trips to the library became more frequent, with the number of books we borrowed increasing with each visit. Even Reshma joined in, by borrowing books and even reading them, though she'd often fall asleep with a book nestled precariously on her face.

We were pleasantly surprised to see the young boy develop into a voracious reader. While I consider myself a connoisseur as a reader, Shlok turned out to be a gourmand at reading. I often tell him that he must read books at a slow pace, relish the experience of how the magic of words helps enrich our imagination. But my son, he reads through books as if there's a race to the last page.

I thought he only skims through the books just to prove to us that he's finished reading a book quicker than us. I quizzed him one day on a book he'd claimed to have read the previous night. Amazingly so, he could retain almost all the details, even calling my bluff when I lied about a certain character's traits.

Reading also lent an impetus to Shlok's expanding vocabulary. Once, he was questioned about his usage of the word 'winsome' in his school project. When he explained the meaning, the very sweet and gracious teacher admitted that Shlok had taught her a new word.

In a span of just a few months, my then nine-year-old son was done catching up with the entire series of Diary of a Wimpy Kid, several of R L Stine's books, Harry Potter, Maze Runner and a lot many more. His favourite though, as yet, is Rick Riordan's Percy Jackson series.

Not all his purportedly 'free' armchair travels while reading are actually free. Shlok charms me into buying some books, while convincing his mom to buy several others. He owns more books than I ever read, when at his age. However, I don't consider buying a book as an expense, but more as an investment.

Heavily influenced by the Percy Jackson book series, our son badgered us endlessly to plan a trip to Greece, till we relented. Yes, this really happened, such are his powers of persuasion. At ten years of age, he made an entire proposal on the pros and cons of visiting Greece for our summer vacation. He had once convinced me to buy a home printer, by making a three-page presentation describing the merits of doing so!

In Athens, we had taken a guided tour across the historical monuments. Our tour guide was beginning to test her tour group's knowledge on Greek mythology, and was pleased to see Shlok's hand raised at each of her questions. He also helped her answer some tricky queries posed to her by other tourists in the group. Seeing him rattling off the names and relations of so many of the Greek Gods, as also their corresponding Roman God equivalents, somebody told us that he sounded like a little tour guide himself.

Towards the end of the tour, the tour guide ended up so charmed by Shlok that she offered him her daughter's hand in marriage, should we consider the proposal. In jest, of course.

We came back mighty impressed with how reading has helped Shlok develop his knowledge base. I proudly told Reshma that our son has inherited my reading genes.

Growing up, I was an avid reader. I was, more often than not, found curled up with a book. However, as I began working life, my interest in reading was relegated to the back seat.

As a child, Reshma was never a reader. Other than the rare chick lit which catches her fancy, she only makes use of reading as an alternative to sleeping pills. Usually four pages is all it takes to put her to sleep.

About six months after our Greece sojourn, I saw Shlok rummaging through his stuff. He was playing with one of his Lego sets and was searching for some missing piece amongst his old toys, when he found an old Rubik's cube in the pile. He asked me to teach him how to solve the cube. I admitted that I didn't know how to even begin solving it, and when he approached Reshma she also replied in a similar manner.

That week, Shlok used up his allotted screen time to learn the basic algorithms of solving Rubik's cube. It took him five days to solve the cube by himself. The second time he tried it, he managed to solve it in four hours.

I heard him complaining that the old cube does not move quick enough for his comfort. I threw a challenge at him. If he could solve the cube, scrambled by me, in less than ten minutes, I'd buy him a new cube. It took him a couple of days, and we rewarded him with a new cube.

I understood that fanning his passion for cubing would help keep him away from screens. It led to a new ritual of sorts. Shlok and I would together set a target for his next achievement, and he'd get to decide his reward, which was invariably another variation of the cube. He solved the cube in less than a minute to win a new 4 X 4 cube.

Of what I can remember, the latest target now stands at less than twenty seconds for the 3 X 3 cube and under two minutes for the 4 X 4 variant.

Thanks to learning the algorithms, Shlok developed some interest in math and algorithms. Also, not restricting himself to only solving the Rubik's cube, Shlok did enough research to know the history behind its invention, the current world record times and reigning champions. He has also taught himself how to dismantle the cube and applying lube in it to make it smoother, and faster.

He tried teaching us how to solve a cube, but both Reshma and I declined his offer. He had also been trying to form a cubing club in his school, searching for fellow cubing enthusiasts.

When Shlok excitedly told Reshma's father about his speedcubing conquests, his grandfather asked him how he became such a smart kid. Shlok replied, "That happened because I've begun thinking out of the box." His grandfather quipped, "You mean, out of the idiot box?"

Tinker, Tailor, Soldier, Sailor

Tinker, Tailor, Soldier, Spy,
What should I become and why?,
So many avenues I espy,
Yet don't know which one to go by.

I asked a senior business associate over dinner, while he was visiting Singapore on business, "So tell me, did you always want to become a banker?"

"Yes," he replied, "Ever since I was a young kid, I always knew I'd grow up to work in a Bank. I would have visions of counting money and managing the teller counter. What about you?" I sidestepped his question by moving on to another topic.

Another evening, "Hey Reshma, weren't you always clear in your mind about career aims, and always focussed all energies to enter the Information Technology industry?" I asked my wife.

"Of course, I had always been fascinated with how computers work, and programming was always my passion. But why are you suddenly so interested to know?"

"Ummm, I have been wondering. Why does our son always seem so confused? He picks up an activity, calls it his passion, loses steam midway, and gives it all up. I was curious to know where this quality of his comes from."

"You, maybe?" she ventured, "fickle father, confused child! Is your career your passion?"

"Not everyone is as lucky as you," I scowled, "You have made your passion for coding your profession. For most people in the world, passion and profession are two different things."

Back to Shlok, he has always reminded me of an old rhyme I once identified with. It began with, "Tinker, Tailor, Soldier, Sailor" and went on to describe several other viable professions. Let me elaborate on why he reminds me of the rhyme.

When Shlok was about seven years old, he was all convinced that he wanted to grow up to be a YouTuber. His first YouTube channel had nineteen subscribers, all of them were relatives and our friends. But alas, his father decided to call curtains on his budding YouTube career. I don't deny that the short stint at making YouTube videos did help him overcome his stutter somewhat.

When he was around eight, even before he became fond of reading, he had decided he would become a writer. He declared thus to not only family, but anyone he conversed with. He had already begun working on a mega manuscript, and had intricately planned how the protagonist would die in book six. He had already promised Reshma's manager, when he met him, that he'd be the lucky one to get as a gift, the first signed copy of Shlok's magnum opus.

By the time my son turned nine, he had caught the gaming bug. He heard stories of people becoming rich by just playing video games, and he wanted in. Again, the screen time ban overturned this promising career aspiration.

When he got pretty fast at solving the Rubik's cube, our son announced his plans of becoming a speedcuber. An elaborate plan went thus: to initially take part in speedcubing competitions, making his mark across continents. Then, set the world record in speedcubing, or come as close as possible to it. Subsequently, once he is famous as a cuber, he'd set up cubing classes and training aspiring cubers. Lastly, he would write a book and then host a YouTube channel, on solving the Rubik's cube.

Shlok was some seven months shy of eleven years of age when I received a call from Panda.

"Let me tell you a story, bro," he began, "There was a young boy who always yearned to be a cricketer, but he was disallowed. His dreams of becoming a poet or accomplished writer were also quashed due to the rigours of life. And then he had a son..."

I interrupted him, "Let's save each other some time, please come to the freaking point."

Turned out that Shlok had called my brother to talk to him about his latest venture. Apparently Shlok wanted to now design a video game, and the decade old boy wanted to pursue an online course on developing games. He'd garnered my brother's support to persuade me into allowing him extra screen time, and to pay the fees for this course.

The certificate evidencing his completing that course enjoys a vantage place of pride on our refrigerator. However, the first line of code on a game has not seen the light of the day yet.

Sometime later, after his game-coding course was completed, Shlok called up my friend who works in the film industry, asking him what writing a movie script entails. My enthusiastic friend shared some movie scripts with Shlok.

"He's just a kid," my friend chided me, "You should be thankful that he is so varied in his interests. Allow him to test out all his aspirations. As a parent, all you can do is give your child a big enough canvas. Let him decide the picture he paints of his life. Truth be told, I am pushing forty years of existence, and I still don't have a clue of where my passions lie. Do you?" I had no answer for my friend, and I ended up pretty much agreeing with his perspective.

Recently, at almost eleven years now, Shlok came to sell to me the idea of buying a gaming console. Watching the screen from a distance, he said, puts much less strain on the eyes as compared to playing a game on the laptop, phone or tablet. My immediate response was that I would buy him the latest gaming console he wanted, as soon as I get promoted, or land a new job opportunity.

Since that day, he took it upon himself to search for a new job for me. A week later, he came to me with a list and a ready speech.

"I have researched on, and shortlisted the best paying jobs in Singapore for you, Papa. The first option is: Equity Trader."

"Son, that won't work for me, as I really don't think I can do that."

"Ummm, how about the next one then? Professional Medical Practitioner."

"For that, I'll need to go back to school, Shlok."

I had to collect my jaw from the floor, where it had dropped, after what he said next.

"Well, then I have just one more left on my list. The only well-paid career option you have is that of a mermaid!"

What an EmbarrASSment!

Many occasions I let you down,
Countless times, you, I did, embarrass,
Yet I continue to be a clown,
Of myself, I always make an ass!

As a parent, it's perfectly acceptable to love your child to the moon and back, and yet at the same time be embarrassed to death by their behaviour in public.

In just over ten years of his existence yet, Shlok has given us many opportunities to experience this emotion.

While I have devoted an entire chapter earlier in this book to Shlok's issue of infant regurgitation, I must speak about his struggles with motion sickness.

He has always had a car fixation. Even as an infant, he would readily jump into the arms of anyone who said they have a car and are going for a spin in it. He loved being taken out for a drive. As a toddler, he'd once hesitated in returning home from my father-in-law's house, because they owned a car, and we didn't. That was one of the reasons why Reshma and I stretched our household budget to buy our first car. It wasn't for our convenience, but for Shlok's love for an outing in the car.

Ever since I can remember, Shlok would do either of two things while in a moving car. On shorter trips, say within the city, involving travel times between ten minutes to under two hours, meant he would fall asleep. That wasn't really a problem, unless the reason for the drive was him insisting that he wants to go out for a drive.

When the travel time increased up to beyond two hours, Shlok sprayed everyone within hurling range with a generous dose of his last meal. I know that several people, me included, have issues when the car is navigating winding roads. But my son had trouble keeping his food in, even when travelling over smooth, straight roads.

Reshma, blessed with keen mother's instinct, would always alert us in time, but only seconds before the vomit hit us.

We were once going for a pilgrimage in a vehicle with some of our relatives. My mother had warned everyone that the route involved winding roads, and everyone must be careful about their issues with nausea. Three-year-old Shlok, though, didn't get the memo. He slept through the 'winding road' part of the journey, but we were prematurely thankful for the averted tragedy.

As soon as we hit the final, straight portion of our journey, Shlok woke up and everyone had to first bathe in his vomit, and hot water immediately after. Reshma and I didn't know where to hide our ashamed faces, though at the same time we couldn't stifle our laughter seeing the comedy of the situation.

Sadly, that was not an isolated incident. I have lost count on the number of times we have had to shell out some hush money to placate vehicle drivers, because Shlok got sick in their cab. He once retched during a jungle safari, and we didn't sight any tigers thereafter. I guess the smell scared the big cats away.

Speaking about cabs, we were once on the way back home from a short vacation, with Shlok complaining about why the trip had to end so soon. He was around five then.

I tried reasoning, "Shlok, you have summer break for a couple of more weeks, but unfortunately Mumma and I need to resume our office."

Shlok asked, "Papa, what work do you do in your office?"

Not very happy with the prospect of resuming work either, I cheerlessly mumbled, "I am a salesperson, so I have to go begging to my clients for their business."

"Begging? You beg? For business? And when I ask you for toys, you tell me that I am a beggar?"

Then turning to his mother, he said, "I have been to Papa's office. He took me there on Children's Day. Lots of other kids were there too. All day in their office Papa and his friends just sing songs, play games and eat pizza, just like we did that day."

The driver of our Uber cab politely excused himself, carefully parked the car by the side of the road, then laughed for a straight five minutes, obviously at my expense.

We were once staying at 'Umaid Bhawan', the most luxurious palace hotel in Jodhpur, a regal city in Rajasthan, a state in India. The hotel staff had arranged a 'heritage walk' for us, along with some other hotel guests. The staff member taking us around, meaning to ask which part of the imposing property we were currently in, said, "Any guesses where we are walking at the moment?"

Six-year-old Shlok could not contain his excitement because he knew the answer. Raising his hand he blurted out, "Rajasthan, we are all in Rajasthan!". There was no applause, the only sounds were of Reshma and me facepalming.

When he was eight years old, we were vacationing at a beach resort in Malaysia; far, far away from Rajasthan. On a tour of the resort's CSR initiative of nature conservation, we were taken to their turtle hatchery. Seeing the newborn turtles trying to move using their flippers, Shlok had to quip aloud, "These are not real turtles, are they? They move like robots!" The only three people not laughing after that were Shlok, Reshma and red-faced me.

As I have learnt the hard way, the reverse also holds true. As an offspring, it is perfectly acceptable to love your parents to the moon and back, and yet at the same time be embarrassed to death by their behaviour in public.

To anyone willing to lend an ear, Shlok never fails to relate an incident involving me getting sick in an airplane toilet. My son was around nine when this shameful incident transpired.

"I was so embarrassed, you know. Papa had thrown up in the airplane toilet. He didn't miss the mirror, the floor, and even the ceiling. The only place he missed vomiting was in the toilet bowl."

I have given so many more opportunities for Shlok to be embarrassed of me. During our trip to Greece, when Shlok was ten, we went for a day cruise in Santorini. Part of the cruise was a trip to the hot springs.

The boat could not go right up to the island, and those who wanted to swim in the warmer waters needed to swim from the boat to the island. The tour operators had categorically warned us that only people who knew how to swim must venture into the deep water.

Shlok insisted on experiencing the waters of the hot spring. While Reshma decided to stayed back, I volunteered to accompany him. I stole a float off some returning women, and we began paddling towards the island, only about fifty metres away. Not too far, but since it was in the open sea the water ran deep.

Around only fifteen metres or so into our swim, I realised that I only knew how to stay afloat, but didn't know how to swim that well. Shlok kept saying "Papa, let's please keep going ahead," but I was frozen at the same spot.

From her vantage point on the boat, Reshma saw me struggling and quickly jumped into the water. Meanwhile, I could only see my entire life flash before my eyes.

Reshma rescued me, and accompanied Shlok for the swim to the island, while I hid myself somewhere back on the boat. Shlok and Reshma are accomplished swimmers; the less said about my swimming abilities, the better. Later, I was thinking I'd rather have drowned in that water, than have lost face in front of my son, and also hundreds of other tourists in exotic Santorini. Since that particular day, I haven't dared to enter even shallow swimming pools around Shlok.

Another recent incident occurred in Shlok's school. My ten-year-old son was selected by his favourite, the French teacher, to make a presentation in French. She was impressed with how soon he picked up the basics, and this was her way of motivating him further.

Reshma couldn't make it to the school that day, so I was appointed to attend the presentation. Standing in front of my son, unable to make out a word of what he was saying, I was nodding like an idiot. An exasperated Shlok had to then make his presentation to someone else's parents, who most probably sympathised with him, for having an illiterate father.

My well-behaved son didn't say so, but I am sure he must be embarrassed, and thinking to himself about his father, "What an embarrassment, no, what an ASS!"

Let's Talk About Sex, Baby

Dad, tell me everything 'bout it,
Tell me of the birds and the bees,
But I'm still little, don't doubt it,
Spare me the gory details, please!

Ever since Shlok was a toddler, I was trying to prepare myself for that inevitable question from him, about the birds and the bees. "Papa, where do all babies come from?" But how does one even begin to explain to their child about it, though? When we were growing up, sex was a taboo topic, not to be spoken about in polite company.

I rationalised, that maybe the socio-cultural thinking during earlier generations frowned upon such discussions, or probably this level of bonding and paternal involvement in children's upbringing was not in vogue back then.

I was always convinced that my son must not learn about sex from questionable sources. These include friends, dirty uncles, smutty books, C-grade soft-porn movies, and porn sites on the web. Essentially, everywhere we learnt our initial lessons of sex from.

If my offspring has questions about this subject, I'd resolved that I must act maturely, and help him understand correctly, and never allow him to get influenced by popular misinformation.

As a brief aside, I had always encouraged him to ask questions. I'd told him, "No question is a stupid question, Shlok. Always be inquisitive." However, ever since he began speaking coherently, he's been bombarding us with incessant questions. Sometimes we joke we should have named him 'Question Mark'.

He was around seven years old, when Reshma and I were arguing over who loves him more.

"Shlok, your Dad loves you more. You are Papa's little man."

Reshma countered, "No, no, you are my baby. You came from my tummy. You were in my tummy before you were even born."

"So what? He was in me before he was in you!" I bit my tongue as soon as I said this.

Inquisitive, Shlok began, "Papa, how was I inside of you?"

"Ummm, before you were in Mummy's tummy, you were inside my heart. I love you so much, Shlok."

Undeterred, he went on, "So if I was in your heart, then how did I land up in Mummy's tummy? Who put me in there, and how?"

I was not prepared for this conversation. I told him I will get back to him. "In a few years, maybe," I muttered under my breath. I would give him one excuse or another to try and defer our man-to-man conversation to a later date.

By the time he turned ten, his classmates had begun murmuring about sex, the chatter around him was growing so loud, that he kept asking me questions about everything he heard from his friends.

One fine day, I took him aside, choosing a time when his mom wasn't around. I began tentatively, but then gained confidence as I saw him nodding.

"So, you mean it really stands erect, like a stick? My friends were saying so." He was involved, asking questions, that meant it was going well, this father and son conversation of ours.

"Oh, so that is what they do, and that is how babies are made!"

I winked at him, smug that I probably did a good job of explaining to him. I had surely learnt well during my MBA on how to structure a discussion.

But it didn't end well. It would be laughably funny only if it didn't make me squirm uncomfortably.

"Wait, so if all babies are made that way, then... it means you and Mumma did that thing?" saying this he made the universal gesture using both his hands, probably how his friends showed him.

"How could you? This is so disgusting. This is how I came to be? I didn't really need to know that my parents did this for me to be born. I am now scarred for life!"

Management Tips from Kids

So many lessons I learnt from adversity,
I hardly learnt them during my good days,
Didn't learn as much at MBA University,
As I did seeing what my kid does and says.

All these past ten-eleven years, I have been struggling, and often failing miserably, to be the best I could at parenting. During the same time, I have been trying to climb the rungs of the corporate ladder. Not sure which of these endeavours I have failed more comprehensively at.

Seeing Shlok grow from an infant to a toddler, I have observed that children can teach us more about management than all the self-help books put together. Actually an entire management skills book can be written just on these learnings. In true management book style, let's explore in brief the salient lessons we can learn from our children.

Life is simple: The communications professor at my business school often said, "Life is simple, but we make it complicated." I've seen this play out several times seeing my son in action.

Shlok once wanted a certain shiny something toy being distributed by someone at an amusement park we were visiting. I was unaware of whether the distribution was free, paid, or only for the selected few people part of a tour group, hence I was hesitant.

He was around three then. He just smiled and told me, "Carry me in your arms, tell that uncle my little son here likes that thing. He will see me and give it to you." As simple as that. I was a bit doubtful, but said to myself, "Nothing ventured, nothing gained." It turned out so, that the genial gentleman was actually distributing those toys as part of a test marketing campaign.

While I was overthinking all that time, my son gave me the simplest of all solutions: to just ask. The evidence of his winning strategy, the shiny toy, was rattling noisily in his victorious hand. It reminded me of the following lines: Ask and you shall receive it; seek and it shall be opened unto you.

Resilience: As adults, we often allow our setbacks to change our worldview. Not children. They always wake up welcoming each day as a new beginning. Never letting sour experiences to impact their attitudes. Children often go to bed crying, bawling. One small nap later, they are back to their wide-eyed curious and cheerful selves.

I have lost count on the number of times Shlok has gone to bed dejected, defeated, sometimes beaten. But he has never woken up in the same morose mood he went to bed with. His 'Good Morning' carries the same enthusiasm each day. Except, of course, on some sleepy school days.

Learning from mistakes: As we go through our respective corporate journeys, we find ourselves making the same mistakes over and over again. Yet, we refuse to learn from several of those mistakes.

Children, on the other hand, are making blunders every day, yet the speed with which they move on by learning from their erroneous ways is commendable. Yes, sometimes it needs gentle persuasion, but haven't we all needed that push to help us change?

Infants learn how to avoid their fingers finding their way into their own eyes. They also learn that involuntarily scratching themselves causes pain to only them. Till they learn that, there's always baby mittens. As an infant, wearing those little mittens, Shlok's cutely moving hands resembled Muhammed Ali's pugilistic moves.

Toddlers learn that inserting their little fingers into a power plug gives a nasty jolt, and don't repeat that mistake ever again. They explore stubbing toes, cutting fingers (not cutting them off), and learn to not do that again.

Older children eventually grow up to learn that the repercussions of bedwetting far outweigh the convenience of doing so.

Persistent selling: I have been a salesperson since as long as I can remember. I understand the different strategies, approaches and nuances of selling as an art, skill and science. But seeing Shlok adopt the strategies taught only in B-school or expensive sales training programmes leaves me bewildered at times.

If one approach doesn't work, he will try another way of charming you, convincing you with a business case. He remains persistent over months. You feel sure you won't give in, but eventually he will find a way where you happily empty your wallet. And not only as a parent am I lauding my own son's wily ways, but I have also heard similar stories of kids conning people by their sheer sales skills.

I am sure many parents will nod in agreement when I propose that 'Tiny Tots Sales College' should be a B-school where little men and women teach older people the astute approaches to making a sale.

Adaptability to change: Companies spend millions of dollars and engage trainers to teach their employees about adapting to transformation projects. Change Management and Transition Management have been buzzwords for quite some time now. But step out of the cubicles, look into the crib, and you'll learn far simpler ways to adapt, with less jargon and more babbling.

Shlok has now spent almost four years outside of India. The speed with which he has adapted to the change of moving to Singapore really amazes me. It also amuses me to no end seeing him converse in French and 'un-Indian accent' English with his friends. With Reshma and me, he speaks in English with an Indian accent. But when he speaks with his grandparents, he turns to chaste Hindi. All these linguistic transitions are instant and seamless.

He is comfortable in business class seats on aircraft, but easily adjusts to bumpy rides on rickety, crowded buses. He doesn't have any qualms sitting on the floor if the sofa is occupied. As adults, we often become so accustomed to our 'comfort zones' that we resist any change and refuse to adapt, whereas our children adjust and adapt so beautifully.

Relationship Management: I was afraid of Shlok being unable to make friends when we moved to Singapore. It warms the cockles of my heart whenever the doorbell rings, and the door opens to little neighbourhood kids asking "Can Shlok come out to play?"

Children engage in furious fights, the likes which if adults get into might lead to a trip to the police station. Yet, in the next few hours the children are back at play, all their differences resolved.

Corporate mavens roll out sham policies in the name of 'Diversity and Inclusion', yet reward bad discriminatory behaviour. Never have I seen children's tiffs becoming racist. Animals, though, are open game. When children fight, their name-calling often involves names of animals, at times even body parts.

I have never seen children disagreeing to be friends with another child on the basis of their skin colour, religious beliefs, socio-economic status, even their dietary preferences. Children are so warm, welcoming and genuinely inclusive.

Our son often comes back home in a rage, having fought with his friend. But when Reshma volunteers to call the other person's mother, he always declines, "No, he is my friend, and we will sort this out." Would adults ever handle office feuds with such maturity?

There have been many occasions where Shlok has pushed Reshma and me into 'hug and make up' endings to our fights. What kids teach us about managing relationships are invaluable lessons indeed.

148

Power dynamics: Wait, this one probably deserves its own chapter.

Power Dynamics

Playing one parent, against the other,
Leaving the poor parents, in a fix,
They seem innocent, to a loving mother,
But all kids are, experts in politics.

Most business school students are conversant with the term 'Power Dynamics'. When I joined the corporate world, as a fresh MBA post-graduate from University, I was advised to align myself favourably with the power centres around me.

Anyone refusing to fully comply with these norms of choosing between differing factions, is penalised, by way of a shortened career at worst, or snail-paced growth at best.

The key operative word here is 'dynamics'. This is because power, or influence, is ever-changing both in terms of centricity as well as intensity. Someone who is a small fry today, might lick his way up to a top management position tomorrow, with the balance of power shifting in his favour. Also, the extent of power someone wields keeps changing.

Did you just flip over to see the cover of the book to make sure? You are still reading about a father's comedic perspective on parenthood.

I have learnt that children make a classic case study on how to navigate power dynamics. I have only one example to learn from, but I am convinced children the world over follow similar stratagems.

Shlok's alignment to either Reshma or me, is based on his need of the hour. Depending on who is favourable to his situation, he will cosy up to either his Mom or Dad.

When I blow hot, he blows cool. If he sees me angry, he'll get conciliatory. If he sees me relenting, he'll try pushing his boundaries just a wee bit more. Pure display of power dynamics. Also, if he wants to make a witty remark, he'll look at me to see if I am encouraging or admonishing him, before deciding whether to complete the wisecrack with a swag, shrug or smile.

He knows that I wield the power on his screen time, so he'll almost always toe the line when I am in a sour mood. He knows Reshma wouldn't intervene if I penalise him by further restricting his screen time.

However, on days when his mom is angry with me, and Shlok sees me at a clear disadvantage, he will go up to her, calm her down, hug her, and make her smile. Reshma, exercising mother's discretion, would end up rewarding him with extra screen time. Those occasions, he'll cock a snook at me.

Children are also experts at capitalising on the lack of communication between parents. Shlok knows that his parents mostly don't exchange notes. So he knows he can get away with obfuscation.

As a recent example of this, my ten-year-old came home from school, to his Mom's instructions to eat an apple as a snack. He wanted to eat a cake, though.

"Papa, is it ok if I eat the cake, I don't feel like eating an apple."

Busy working on my office laptop, I responded with, "Shlok please don't bother me. Your mother asked me to tell you to eat an apple, do check with her."

I heard him talking to his mother on the phone, and resumed my work.

"Papa, Mumma told me she is ok with me eating the cake now, maybe if I eat the apple later." Saying this, he scurried over to the fridge.

That evening, both Reshma and I blamed each other for allowing him to wipe off that sinful cake. Apparently Shlok had caught Reshma at a busy moment in office and she'd told him, "I am fine with you eating whatever you want, if your Dad says yes."

This was only one of many such instances. I have seen Shlok leverage on this lack of detailed communication between Reshma and me several times, to his advantage.

One day, lending me a glimpse into his knowledge of power dynamics and power politics, my ten-year-old son explained our domestic hierarchy to me.

"You see, Papa, you are like my boss. But I know that Mumma has some power over you. But that's only here in Singapore. Back in India, my uncles and aunt are older to you guys. But as per our culture, the supreme court in our family is grandmother."

"So, like, I know, if I really, really want something, I know whom to give a call to, so you can't refuse." He plain winked at my flabbergasted expression.

Culture: Confluence or Confusion

Pray tell me, dear Daddy of mine,
What do different cultures say?
One man's meat is, I opine,
Another man's poison, if I may.

When we moved from India to Singapore, Shlok was seven years old. Today he is a little shy of eleven. If we discount for the first three as his formative years, then he has spent roughly half his life in India, with the rest in Singapore.

His life has been an interesting mix of the hubbub in the bylanes of Mumbai's suburbs and the bustle of an international hub that Singapore is.

In comparison, Reshma and I have spent almost all our thirty nine years in India. Reshma jokes that amongst the three of us, I have found it most difficult to understand the Singlish spoken in Singapore.

Our hope was that Shlok would gather a confluence of the variety of rich cultures he has been exposed to. While he has assimilated very well the commonalities and the stark differences between these two megacities; he does stumble sometimes, confused over the cultural differences.

Shlok tries his best to be a good ambassador for the Indian cultural and value system, but he surely misses the omnipresent guidance of his grandparents, especially with both his parents busy working.

When Shlok was nine, he was chosen to portray the role of Lord Ram in a school play based on the Indian epic Ramayan, as part of their Diwali festivities. One evening, he was memorising his lines when I heard some obvious mispronunciations.

"Shlok," I began my diatribe, "you are pronouncing these names incorrectly. The English spelling of some Indian words, and their pronunciation, are not how Indians spell and pronounce them. I'd expect you, coming from India, to pronounce their names in the correct manner."

"The waters of the holy river Ganga are probably pronounced as 'Gan-Jess' in other parts of the world, but Indians pronounce it as 'Gung-gays'. Similarly, in Northern India people don't pronounce the trailing 'A' in the spellings of religious figures. Lord 'Rama' must be pronounced as just Lord 'Raam', and King 'Dashratha' is pronounced as King 'Dashrath'. I refuse to spell it as 'Rama' or 'Ramayana', preferring instead the versions which I feel are correct, as 'Ram' and 'Ramayan'. In my opinion, 'Yoga' should be just 'Yog'. Capisce?"

He heard me out quietly, and then frustrated at the contradictions, blurted, "Why are we Indians like this? Why can't we pronounce the words just like we spell them? Now can you please tell me whether I must address the girl playing my wife's part in the play as 'Sita', or plainly just 'Sit'?"

I had to bite my tongue and hide my face, while Reshma patiently explained to him that Goddess Sita's name is indeed pronounced as Sita.

Ten-year-old Shlok was once given an assignment in school. The music teacher had asked his class to bring in samples of songs which reflect the culture of the countries they hail from.

To be fair to him, our son had approached both his parents for some guidance. I was struggling with some urgent work, so I waved at him to stay away. His mom was on back-to-back conference calls. She too, shooed him out from her home office.

This left him with only the internet for research. We all know how helpful that can turn out to be.

Half an hour later, I was on a temporary respite from the arduous task I was working on. So I thought I'd go check on my son in his room. I was aghast to hear him recording, in his voice, a song from a Bollywood blockbuster from my childhood days.

He was singing 'Jumma chumma de de' from the legendary Indian actor Amitabh Bachchan's hit multi-starrer movie 'Hum'. Coincidentally, the film was released in 1991, when Reshma and I were ten years old.

The song 'Jumma chumma de de' was quite a rage back then. To put things into perspective, in the song, lyrics loosely translated, the protagonist is asking his lady love, named Jumma, for a kiss. She'd apparently promised him last Friday that she'd kiss him next Friday. And since it was now the agreed Friday, Amitabh came to her singing with lustful gusto to demand what was owed to him.

I was enraged, "You told me you were to submit a song reflecting Indian culture. You should either choose a song describing the varied heritage of Indian culture, or some song praising Indian value system. What part of this song 'Jumma chumma' asking for a kiss, reflects Indian culture for you, Shlok?"

"Don't get too worked up Daddy-O," Shlok began to explain, "I read it here on Google that the song is part of pop 'culture' amongst generations of moviegoers in India. I have heard you and Mumma humming along when this song played while watching a rerun of the movie in which it figures. 'Hum' was the movie I think."

"Shlok, just because the song was a big hit, and your parents sing along when it plays, doesn't mean it is any which way indicative of Indian culture." The anger in me was simmering.

"Whatevs, Pops. I might decide on another song, but you must know that I am the only Indian in my class. My music teacher is a Canadian. Nobody other than me understands a word of Hindi. Who can prove that the song I chose doesn't sing paeans in the glory of India's rich cultural heritage?"

What Patriotism?

The shrinking world, is now a global village,
And all borders are just imaginary lines,
Why is my questioning patriotism, sacrilege,
Why, my Dad, for distant lands, pines?

He continued, "While on songs, Papa, whenever you hear yesteryear songs, you always hum along with a smile. When you listen to a humdinger of a dance number, you even try a jig. However, if you listen to an Indian patriotic song, or even when you attempt to sing one, why do I unfailingly see you dabbing your eyes with a hanky, if not openly whimpering?"

Shlok's observations were pretty astute. He added, "And this has nothing to do with moving away from India. I vividly remember seeing you cry over patriotic songs even when we were in India. The only other time I have seen you bawl inexplicably was when your hero Sachin Tendulkar retired from playing cricket. I was too young to know why, hence couldn't belt out Elvis' 'Don't cry Daddy'. But seriously, why do you cry?"

I smiled, "Let me take the Sachin question first. I'd first seen him play cricket when I was probably as young as you are now. Ten or eleven years old, perhaps. He went on to play cricket, representing India, for 24 years, winning innumerable accolades. For countless people my age, Sachin Tendulkar's retirement was not only the end of an illustrious era, but also the veritable end of our own childhood. These things can make grown men cry; you know. Plus, for millions of cricket lovers in India, including me, the game of cricket is like a religion, and Sachin Tendulkar, venerable God."

I did not miss seeing his eyes rolling, but I could understand that what is holy for me probably doesn't hold the same significance for most others.

"On to your observation on India, Shlok," I sighed, "Indians are considered amongst the most patriotic people. India receives the largest amount of inward remittance in the world, from its huge diaspora of sons and daughters living abroad."

"But that is also because of high interest rates," he interjected, putting up a hand, "I heard my teacher say so."

"Hey, lots of Indian expatriates have family back home, and associated expenses," I countered, "so remittance in any form, whether expense or investment, is still good money."

"Plus, Shlok, please try and understand this fact," I explained, "Everyone on earth loves their country, whether they stay there or elsewhere. It's called patriotism. Don't get me wrong, I am incredibly impressed with Singapore, and I love this place a lot too."

Shlok acted as if he was reeling in a whopper of a prize catch, "Patriotism, what patriotism, Dad? My teacher says there are around 200 countries in the world, and the education system in most countries is designed to, what's the word? Yes, indoctrinate. To indoctrinate their citizens with the thought that their particular country is the best in the world. He says, but the world is now a global village."

I shirked away from the debate saying, "Wow, your school is teaching you big words. I am glad your vocabulary is expanding. Run along now, I have some emails to respond to."

On another occasion, I asked my almost eleven-year-old son, "Shlok, my career is in a bit of a flux situation. Lots of office politics. If we were to move, what would you think about going back to India?"

"I like it here, Papa," He flinched, but composed himself before responding, "I find that most of the places I've seen in India can be summed up in two words. 'Crowded', and 'Dirty'. Please don't think of me as a hoity toity. I totally love the food in India. I like India. Most of the people I love either stay in India or are from there. But this is what I observed."

I was shell-shocked. "NO! Shlok, you cannot talk like this! India is our country. It has some challenges, yes, but that doesn't make it any less lovable."

"Look at it this way," I tried drawing an analogy, "try thinking of country as a mother. Your mother has some flaws, but you still love her unconditionally, don't you?" He nodded.

"Similarly, India is my motherland, and a mother to me," I continued the metaphor, "Just like I love my mother, your grandmother, to nuts, I am crazily in love with India as well. India, Shlok, is also my mother." I was in tears by then, and furiously wiping away the streams running down my wet cheeks.

Only an innocent child can make a crying person laugh in an instant. Shlok threw his hands up, eyes wide open in shock, "You mean, that in addition to my grandmother, my grandfather also got married to India?"

Generation Zee

Our opposing opinions, thought differentiation,
Can be blamed on generational gap,
Deal with it, I'm the latter generation,
Why my quick wit then, it does you, zap?

I n the five years that Shlok spent under the near-exclusive tutelage of my mother, she imparted to him the strongly founded values of the typical Indian middle class family. Respect to elders, polite tones and charitable behaviour are global hallmarks of a healthy middle class culture.

A while after moving to Singapore, we began seeing some changes in his behaviour. Initially, we'd credited this newfound assertiveness to the rigours of dealing with change. But his volume, and what we perceived as him being obdurate and argumentative, went on increasing.

"It is this exposure to western culture from that international school you enrolled him into, that is bringing out the brute in him. He needs to learn more of Asian culture." This was from a well-meaning Asian colleague of mine.

I politely explained that cultures globally look down upon boorish behaviour. "The school is perfectly fine, and their culture itself is very respectful, warm and welcoming just like Singapore itself."

We were seated in the large boardroom in our office, awaiting a conference call to begin.

"But I agree that cultural differences do exist," our American colleague joined the discussion, "I have stayed in the USA and also in Singapore. I can see the difference between Western and Asian cultures."

"In the western culture," He stressed with his signature southern drawl, "The focus begins with self, 'Me'. When my needs are met, I give to the family. Only if my family approves do I contribute to the society at large. With Asians, however, the locus of control lies with society. After society, I concentrate on family. Only after the family is fully sated, do I think about myself. Both cultures are different, and neither is wrong where they come from."

Another colleague of ours invited herself into the conversation. "Well explained, buddy. I like the interesting distinctions you draw. But how does it help solve our friend's question here?"

Offering an answer, she continued, "The issue at hand is not about cultural difference at play, but just plain old generation gap. What you see as screaming by your little one, is his way of asserting himself as a growing up child. We did the same way with our parents, but have forgotten our times, maybe. My father tells me I would have infamous shouting matches with him when I was young. I have three of my own to know what you describe as your kid's changed behaviour."

We had to curtail our conversation as the conference call crackled to a start.

I understood this concept better much later, when Reshma and Shlok once engaged in their own loud screaming match.

"Shlok," she bellowed, "I am from the IT industry, I very well know how to deal with some silly Insta privacy settings. You are only ten yet and still learning."

"Mumma," his riposte was loud too, "Just because I am your son doesn't mean that you can't learn a thing or two from me."

Reshma left in a huff, saying she didn't like being spoken to like that. I knew I was to become the peacemaker.

I began in a soft tone. "Shlok, we come from a generation where we had a solitary rotary phone for several houses. Black and white television sets were considered a luxury. We saw the tape cassette evolve into a CD, and then the takeover by the pen drive, finally to streaming music. We've seen the advent of the digital age, and adopted it wilfully. Your mom is actually making bots, spearheading machine learning and Artificial Intelligence technology at her workplace."

"I should also tell you, that probably we are the last generation which will be respectful towards our parents. Your generation thinks that they are an entitled lot, and equal to, if not better than, your elders." I could sense my emotions, and my volume, rising.

"Papa, just because we assert our opinions doesn't make us disrespectful at all. I understand you were expected to behave in a certain way around your parents. Our generation thinks differently. That doesn't mean we don't love our parents. You and Mumma were born in which year, 1980? You're probably a cusp between Generation X and the Millennials, or whichever wave was prevalent in India when you were born. No disrespect, but I am Generation Z, deal with it." He pronounced 'Z' as 'Zee'.

"And about the digital part, please," his finishing move knocked me out, "you have to accept this as fact, that you and mom are digital immigrants. I was born in it; I am a digital native."

Livin' on a Prayer

Holding your hands, as I wisely speak,
Give you hope and strength, I can,
I'm growing up quick, no longer am weak,
Child is, indeed, the father of man!

There is no doubt in my mind that 'Gen Z', however you choose to pronounce the letter, is savvier than we were. I would credit this to the sheer exposure they have, compared to us in our childhood. My son has the luxury of being born in an age where information is accessible quicker than you can finish saying 'Ok Google'.

I have experienced this first-hand. I was pursuing an online course on new financial technologies, and sensed my ten-year-old son peeking over my shoulder.

"Papa, are you learning about the Dark Web? I can explain it to you."

Shlok then went on to expound the facets of the dark web, some of which weren't even covered in the training video. I began doubting if he's been surfing the dark web, when he assured me that he doesn't have the 'TOR' browser to access the dark web, and that they'd been taught about it at school.

I know that probably every ten-year-old kid around the globe behaves in a similarly smug, knowledgeable, and assertive manner. It should be no surprise. What amuses me is how my son has grown up from the little newborn placed into my tentative hands.

The infant spouting a cute 'Agoo' is now big enough to ask me about my knowledge of the Quantum Realm. I'd honestly started questioning my education, my Bachelor of Science majoring in Physics, over this query of his, when I was assured by a friend that this term comes from a Hollywood movie. Phew!

The young Shlok, whose dirty diapers were changed by me. Ok, just that one time, but yeah. That little toddler is now grown up enough to be ashamed of coming out of the bathroom naked. He also expresses embarrassment over being lovingly spoken to in a babbling tongue by his mom, and takes offence when some Singaporean aunty calls him 'Baby'.

A little boy, who everyone was concerned about not speaking, now talks incessantly and we have to ask him to speak less. My mom, when apprised that Shlok will be in grade 6 coming academic year, expressed her surprise with, "How did he grow up so soon?"

My 'wounded soldier' is almost eleven years old and teaches me words like 'deuteragonist'. Learning a new word from your offspring makes you feel humbled and proud at the same time.

One day, our son sensed that both his parents were desperately praying for a new lease of life in our respective careers. He called an urgent family conference, and played Bon Jovi's "Livin' on a prayer" aloud on his iPad. The inspirational lyrics worked like magic. It immediately became our family's anthem for quite some time.

On another occasion, he came up to me and told me something which left me in tears, "I know you have been struggling with issues at your office. But you never bring your troubles home. I really admire the way you keep smiling all the time, even during the hardest of times. I love you a lot."

Hearing such mature words from him, at a tender age of ten, often leaves us surprised.

Sometimes, when we are trying to explain something to him, he'll interject with, "But Mumma, Papa, I already know that. You know I wasn't born yesterday?"

Our immediate response to that is a wistful, "Oh, but it only feels like just yesterday, when you were born, my little baby!"

Monkey See, Monkey Do

Speak pages of pedagogy, you may,
Will not, their characters, shape,
'Tis what you do, and not what you say,
Is just what your children will ape!

Motherhood, in my opinion, is like learning to drive a car. You start tentatively. Once you get the hang of all gears or buttons, it is all about judgement, or mother's instinct. Reshma nods with a smile, agreeing with my assessment of motherhood.

Fatherhood, on the other hand, is like sitting on a new roller coaster for the first time. You just sit, holding white-knuckle tight. The ride takes you around turns, bends and loops. All you can do is look around to see if something has fallen, or try to avoid the vomit being hurled all around you.

But just parents alone are not enough, they say, it takes a village to give a child a good upbringing. We have been fortunate that for the first seven of Shlok's formative years we had a strong support system of our family, friends and friendly neighbours. If my mother was indisposed awhile or travelling, Reshma's mom was always ready to help look after Shlok. We have lost count on the number of times Reshma's youngest sister stayed weekends with us, to take care of her nephew and relieve an overworked Reshma. Resultantly, his aunt is on top of the list of Shlok's most loved people.

As parents, we have learnt from our parents, and many other parents, the fine art of parenting. Parenting is essentially all about learning by trial and error. We make mistakes, learn from them, and try teaching our children the lessons we learnt.

Someone once told us that it is not what you tell your children to do, that they imbibe. They see what you say and do, and follow in your footsteps. Children ape your behaviour as parents.

"It is a simple old case of 'monkey see, monkey do', that's how children are. As an example, you can't expect your offspring to be reading a book just because you asked them to. They'll pick up reading if reading is a habit with their parents."

I wish to become a good role model for my son, and I always strive to become the best version of 'Shlok's Dad' I can be. I earnestly hope the value system we try to inculcate in our son holds him in good stead, especially in the times I am no longer around to guide him.

Reshma and I have always followed a principle of celebrating bad days. Our theory is that while we must always celebrate happy occasions, we must never forget the lessons our bad days teach us. Good days give us happiness, while bad days build character.

Shlok has always seen us celebrating bad days but we never knew whether our philosophy would have any impact on our son.

Recently, our almost eleven-year-old son expressed that he wanted to run for student council in his school. It was evident to Reshma and me, that he ran a slim chance. He had newly transferred to another campus of the school, and barely knew anyone there. The other contenders, of course, would have many more friends and were obviously popular. We, however, refrained from discouraging him from running for the student council.

It is characteristic of Shlok to shun comfort zones, and he keeps challenging himself. So he wrote a short speech, sought help from me to fine-tune it, and went with his best smile on the day of the election.

Reshma and I were deliberating over how badly he would take the defeat. That afternoon, we were pleased to see that our upbringing is building firm foundations of a strong value system in our son. The proverbial apple has fallen right next to the tree.

Shlok wrote an email to us, "I lost the elections. I'll celebrate by eating three scoops of ice cream today."

Wrapping Up

He tried speaking while stuffing his mouth with cake, "Hey, brother, thanks for the cake. It is your son's birthday, is it? He's turned eleven, hasn't he? Did you know they call it as tweens, or something like that, nowadays? This age from ten to twelve. Mmmm, nice cake. I like the cake's design too, 'Eleven' from 'Stranger Things', am I right?"

I'd brought some leftover birthday cake to share with my office pals. A senior colleague, ten years my senior in age as well, was speaking to me. I really look up to him, because though he is pushing fifty, he has the enthusiastic attitude of an eighteen-year-old, and is very generous with good advice. I also look up to him because he is a full four inches taller.

"So you think your growing up pains are over, dude? Your son is a big boy now? Wait till your trials actually begin, when he is in his teens. My son is fifteen, and refuses to acknowledge me as a father. He goes around to some gaming tournaments with his friends, and wins real money. The only leverage I had over him was, of course, money. Brace yourself for the testing teens. Enjoy it while he's still an obedient child."

Looking back at the past decade or so, I realise that trying to learn how to be a good father has also taught me invaluable life lessons, some of which I've tried to share over the course of this book.

If I survive his teens, I might attempt to write about my experiences of seeing my little boy growing up into a young man.

Thanks for reading.

Signing off...

Shlok's Dad.

Acknowledgements

There is a popular internet meme which goes something like this: If I tell you I'll do something, I'll do it. You don't have to keep reminding me every six months.

Ever since we've known each other, Reshma has been insisting that I must write. Anything, a blog, a short story, a novel, whatever. She's not been the first one to say so. My favourite school teacher, Rekha Shahani, saw the spark in me too. My brothers, Bajju and Pawan, were ever-encouraging. My mother, Kamla (we just call her Mummy), always inspires me to write poetry like her.

However, Reshma has been incessantly nagging me to write, and so deserves most plaudits for being persistent in pushing me. The germ of an idea for this book sprouted in 2014, when I wrote the first five lines. It took till October of 2020 for Reshma to convince me to pick it up again, and finish it!

The amazing people who agreed to go through my manuscript, and gave me invaluable feedback, cannot be thanked enough. They convinced me that what I had jotted down from memory, was worth publishing, as it is a story which deserves to be shared with many others. Loads of love and gratitude to Priyanka Lalwani, Nandini Jhaveri, Avinash Singh, Aleman Muralidhar, Meghna Sharma, Rekha Shahani Jagasia, Anil Jain, Vishal Joshi. It does take an army to drive me into action; led, of course, by my wife! Reshma also deserves extra credit for sketching on paper my vision for the book cover.

Needless to say, as the headliner of this effort, Shlok deserves the deepest words of gratitude: for allowing me to tell his story; for competing with me to write a book so I could be goaded to complete (and in decent time too); for being his awesome, witty and funny self and hence giving me enough fodder and funny incidents to write about.

Shlok, I LOVE YOU! ♥

About the Author

Vivek Sharma is a B.Sc. in Physics, and holds an MBA in Finance, but recalls nothing in detail about both subjects. He distinctly remembers cutting classes and reading books or composing poetry, when not whiling away time humming Bollywood songs.

He claims to be climbing the rungs of the corporate ladder, as an international Banker, but has been struggling to learn the ropes of parenting since October 2009.

His designation, since then, has been - Shlok's Dad. With the onset of COVID-19, his wife has conferred upon him the additional title of Shlok's Mom (part-time).

With this book, Vivek hopes to begin a dialogue on the funny and not-so-funny learnings from parenthood in general, and fatherhood in particular. If any part of this book has touched you emotionally, has reminded you of a child's growing-up days, made you smile or laugh, Vivek would be delighted to hear about it from you. He can be reached on:

Email shloksdad@gmail.com

Twitter @ShloksDad

Facebook facebook.com/ShloksDad

Made in the USA
Las Vegas, NV
30 January 2021

16846513R00109